Furnace Creek

By the same author

Montana Moon
Blackfeet Country
Sage City
Devil's Canyon
The Linkman
The Nighthawk

FURNACE CREEK

CHARLES BURNHAM

ROBERT HALE • LONDON

© *Charles Burnham 1995*
First published in Great Britain 1995

ISBN 0 7090 5696 6

Robert Hale Limited
Clerkenwell House
Clerkenwell Green
London EC1R 0HT

The right of Charles Burnham to be identified as author of this work has been asserted by him in accordance with the Copyright, Designs and Patents Act 1988.

Printed and bound in Great Britain by
WBC Book Manufacturers Limited, Bridgend, Glamorgan.

1
PUEBLO MUERTE

During the summer the desert temperature reached 120° Fahrenheit and stayed there day and night. During the winter it might drop to about 90° or 100°.

Vegetation was sparse, roads into the Furnace Creek country were practically non-existent. There were trails, mostly those used by animals going to and from water, which was available in only a few places, usually miles apart.

The Furnace Creek country was well below sea level; it had scatterings of skeletons both animal and human, the older of which had usually been covered with sand and silt by winds that regularly added to the inhospitableness of the area. An early-day Frenchman who had crossed the territory called it *purgatoire*, which later travellers had corrupted to purgatory.

The natural inhabitants of this place were lizards, snakes – mostly poisonous – gila monsters, the occasional desert fox and infrequently drawn by the scent of a carcass, coyotes.

Waterholes, not uncommonly poisonous, were scarce. At some of them skeletons were the only warning of poison.

The country was shunned by everyone who had ever ventured far into it. If there had ever been inhabitants of the Furnace Creek country it had to have been eons earlier when, perhaps, the place had not been as hostile to life, but that had to be conjecture. If they had ever lived here for long in aboriginal communities there were no scattered and crumbling ruins to suggest it.

In distant towns and villages it was said that even buzzards flying over it had to carry food with them.

Furnace Creek, from which the desert derived its name, came out of the earth about thirty miles northward. At its source the water was too hot to touch, but eventually, miles southward, it cooled to a degree not unlike warm bath water, and that far south it was drinkable. The problem was that where Furnace Creek reached the desert was approximately in the centre. Too distant for riders to people with wagons to reach it before dying of thirst.

One variety of dweller of this lost world which throve there were tiny birds called cactus wrens. Other inhabitants such as rattlesnakes and a deadly poisonous, ugly, large lizard known as the gila monster, a sluggish, multi-coloured creature, survived on diets ranging from insects to the sinewy carcasses of dead creatures. There was no antidote for the gila monster's poisonous bite. However, they did not attack unless provoked, and anyone wearing cowhide boots reaching just below the knee, could stamp the animal to death or simply kick it out of the way.

Vegetation was limited to bitter-tasting, ground hugging plants not unlike sage, but they were not numerous. Of trees there were none, not in the desert itself,

Furnace Creek

but on its bordering territory there were trees. There were also what remained of adobe ruins, some two-storeys high. Whoever those ancient people had been they had created their communities close to water. There were a number of dry creekbeds where once water had coursed. It may have been that when the creeks dried up the *Anasazi* had abandoned their settlements.

One of those ruins, still habitable, had an ancient dug well. One of these places, known locally by its old Spanish name of *muerto pueblo*, could have derived its name from the early Spanish explorers having found dead Indians at the settlement. Here the rare traveller could find a place to rest, safe from pursuit and, if such people knew the desert to the south they could handily elude pursuers. Very rarely did manhunters have the knowledge or the inclination to go very far into the desert. They did not have to possess great intelligence. All that was required for them to heed instinctive warnings was to sit their horses on one of the ridges and look out over the vastness of the lifeless and deadly place still referred to as purgatory.

That the prehistoric *pueblo* had been inhabited from time to time was indicated by discarded tins, ash from dead cooking fires, and signs of horses which could graze north of the pueblo where tough grass flourished.

The country surrounding the desert, except southward, had trees, grass and game. Southward the desert ran all the way down into Mexico. Those who had crossed it down there called it *jornada del muerto*. The journey of death.

North and east the countryside was not much different from other livestock territory. Westerly, the land was poor and the villages poorer.

During periods of drought elsewhere cattlemen drove herds to the vicinity of the pueblo, but never close enough to cause anxiety among inhabitants, if there were any. Cattlemen restrained their animals from drifting beyond the low ridges down into the desert.

They also watched them carefully; there were still Indians in the territory who avoided the old pueblo for reasons of hand-me-down superstition, but they had no inhibition against running off a few head of cattle.

They were said to be Navajo, Zuni, even Apaches and Kiowas, but miscegenation among Mexicans, other tribes and whites, had left very few pure bloods.

They lived by raiding, moved camps often, never lingered in areas where they could not see in all directions. They were as elusive as ghosts.

The army had made sweeps, had caught a few to be returned to reservations, but these had been mostly the old, the very young and those who did not own horses.

It was a trio of these brigand Indians who, from a distance, had seen smoke rising from the pueblo and had carried this information to their clansmen, but nothing short of an imminent massacre would induce the hideout marauders to go close to the pueblo. Legend said it was haunted by *fantasmas* and when the wind blew through its doorless and windowless openings, one could hear the cries of the tormented.

Their forefathers had lived off the effects of wagoners who had tried to cross the desert. From them they had also acquired the horses, oxen and mules still alive after the wagoners were not.

But those days had passed. Now they survived by hunting, stealing where not not even the *rurales* made

Furnace Creek

an effort to fight them.

The entire Furnace Creek country was inhospitable; deadly. In such an environment only one thing mattered: survival.

Death was never more than an arm's-length away in one of many forms. It was a deathly silent area where old John Beeson stood one pink dawn looking out over the dead desert and spoke to the man at his side, who was not as old. Beeson said, 'That's got to be what hell looks like.'

His companion nodded. 'How far down yonder is Messico?'

Old John settled a cud before answering. 'Maybe sixty miles as the crow flies, but a crow'd drop dead out of the sky if he tried it. We'll circle around easterly.' John pocketed the plug of tobacco before adding more. 'An' that'll be a considerable distance – maybe a week or ten days.'

The younger man, tall and lean, continued to look southward. In the pink dawn it did not look too formidable. He turned back toward the pueblo to make a fire and use their one small can to mix well-water with the hard strips of pepper-cured jerky for their breakfast.

Old John went northward to look at their animals. The horses were hobbled with chain restraints, the kind people used in country like this where leather hobbled horses disappeared in the night.

When he returned the sun was climbing. It had been a hot night and would now become an even hotter day.

Tom Ellison piled their two tin plates with food, kicked aside the saddle-bags where he intended to sit and John looked up. 'Show some respect for them saddle-bags,' he said. 'There's a lot of money inside.'

Furnace Creek

The lanky man sat down, grunted and held a poised spoon as he looked across the tiny fire. 'Any sign?' he asked.

John was spooning in food and did not reply for some time, then all he said was, 'Some. The button-toed moccasins.'

'How many?'

'Three; not very close. Watchin' I'd say. Scoutin' us up.' John ran a sleeve across his lips. 'Like I told you, they got fear of this set of mud rooms. Last time I come through here I met an old gaffer over in a village westerly. He told me about the In'ians. He didn't know what tribe they are, an' it didn't matter. As long as we stay close they won't bother us.'

Tom, the lanky younger man said dryly, 'I'm not worried for us. It's the horses. If a man got set afoot in this country he might want to go north an' find the posse riders. Anything's better'n starving.'

John raided the plate, poured the juice down, wiped his face again and put the plate aside. 'You worry too much,' he said. 'We'll make it, stay down in Messico for a few months then come back.'

The younger man also tipped up his plate. Afterwards he said, 'California; you ever hear of the Barbary Coast out there? Money like dirt, decent places to sleep up off the ground –'

'An' police thicker'n hair on a dog's back,' Beeson said, groping for his plug. 'They got the telegraph out there. After we waited 'em out down yonder you'd do better to head for Missouri or Nebraska . . . maybe Texas. I've been to the Big Bend country down there. Even the army can't get you; there's too many red-necks who shoot at anythin' wearin' blue.'

Furnace Creek

'Is that where you're going?'

'Not this time. I've waited 'em out down there twice. A man's safe enough but that's the wildest, ruggedest piece of country I've ever seen. This time I'm goin' where I never been before. Oregon. What I've heard it's got miles of grazin' country, plenty of water, plenty of game an' not too many people.'

The younger man held up his hand, arose, went to the door and looked out. Without facing back around he said, 'Riders.'

The older man also arose and went to look northward. It looked like eight or ten of them. They weren't riding south toward the pueblo, they were riding due east in the direction of some timbered land where there were piles of prehistoric rock.

John made his judgment. 'Possemen. Likely they lost horses an' are In'ian hunting.' Under the circumstances it was a reasonable guess but it was wrong.

Two days later when John went to look at the horses, he faded behind an eroded wall of ancient adobe. There were three men standing with their hobbled animals. The had reins in their left hands as they led their own riding stock around the hobbled horses.

It was too far for John to hear what was being said but it inclined him to cut their rest sort. He waited until the strangers got a-horseback then scuttled back to the adobe to tell the younger man what he had seen.

The lanky man listened, went to peer out the doorway, saw nothing and returned. 'Which way did they go?'

'West.'

'Then we better go east – or south. They just looked at the horses?'

'Yeah, just walked around 'em.'

The lanky man said, 'Readin' brands?'

John shrugged. 'What difference would that make? Them are Wyoming brands.'

The younger man looked steadily at Beeson. 'You been to the towns beyond the desert?'

'Yes. There's only one you could call a town. The others is shack settlements.'

'Does that town have a telegraph?'

Beeson hung fire. Even when he answered it was only to nod his head.

The younger man looked in the direction of their bedrolls and saddlery. 'Before daylight tomorrow, John. Goin' due south would be my choice.'

John stood gazing at the lanky man. 'You never been down there or you wouldn't have said that.'

'Sixty miles to the border? We can do it maybe two days, most likely three.'

Beeson went to sit on his bedroll before speaking again. 'You can't push horses down there, an' there's no water you can drink until you get dang near to the border. I told you, there's no way to make it due south. I've been down there. A damned snake's got to carry food with him, and even then between here'n there most of the water is poisonous.'

Tom Ellison did not relent easily. 'We could be fifteen miles by sunup if we started right now.'

John's patience was wearing thin. He said, 'We could divvy up right now'n you can go south. Me, I'll go east.'

A horse whinnied. Both men went to the door, but there was no sign of a horse. No sign of anything. Tom started to move outside. John caught his sleeve to hold

Furnace Creek

him back. 'That's the oldest trick in the world. Make a man get curious enough to go out into plain sight.'

There was one doorway and one window-hole. The window-hole was in the south wall. They went over there and still the area showed no movement of any kind.

One thing they were certain about; that horse had not been one of their own. Their animals were some distance northward. Too far for a whinny to be heard.

Tom moved restlessly, freed the tie-down thong on his holstered Colt peeked out the openings several more times until John said, 'Set! If they're out there you pacin' up and down'll get their attention one way or another.'

For John Beeson, who had been down here before as well as elsewhere in tomahawk country, that hadn't been a horse. It had been some scouting-up Indian. They could call a bird down out of a tree, imitate a snake's rattle good enough to fool snakes. Mimicking a horse was child's play.

He could be wrong of course; he'd been wrong other times, but given the circumstances and the situation he doubted that he was wrong this time.

He said very little until dusk settled, then, after he ate cold jerky he loosened the tie-down over his holstered Colt and jerked his head.

They went to the doorway. John said, 'Be quiet.' They stood in motionless silence so long Tom got restless, but he remained quiet and motionless until John brushed his arm and slipped outside into the lowering darkness. They went carefully and without noise in the direction of their horses. At one point Tom whispered, 'I don't like the notion of leavin' them saddle-bags back there.'

The older man's reply to that was succinct. 'Money won't do you no good if you're dead. In this country bein' afoot's the same thing.'

'But hell, if they was outlaws an' come back to search the adobe –'

'It ain't the fellers we saw on horseback. Be quiet!'

They sifted through increasing darkness until they were in the area where they had left the horses. For a moment John's heart sank. He could not see the horses.

They sashayed, covering considerable ground and right up to the moment he caught sight of movement, John was beginning to regret the life he had chosen.

The horses raised their heads. It was dark and they had seen nothing, but two-legged things who hadn't been able to bathe in many days projected a gamey scent animals could detect.

They went around the horses before approaching them. That too was Beeson's idea. He hadn't come down in the last rain by about fifty years.

The animals were full as ticks and while grass and browse allowed animals to hold their own in weight and strength, anyone, particularly outlaws, knew better than to rely on grazing for durability. Using horses required grain.

Nevertheless these animals had been steadily recuperating from their recent long, hard ride to the Furnace Creek country. They'd had many days to recover and were in passably good condition, and they were alert. They probably identified their owners by scent, but whether that was so or not they made no effort to hop clear when John and his lanky companion approached them.

John made a brief inspection of the animals and their hobbles, then, as he stood up he said, 'Son of a bitch!' and started back to the adobe. He made no attempt to explain his abrupt reversal nor did he employ any of the wariness he had employed in getting up there.

2
DISASTER

His hunch was right, he had fallen for one of the oldest tricks in the world: the saddle-bags were gone!

Tom sat on a bedroll looking at his partner without speaking. He'd said leaving the saddle-bags unguarded worried him. He did not have to repeat it. John cursed the gloom. He had learned survival over the years but it was impossible to read sign without light.

He left the adobe. Tom Ellison continued to sit glumly. He had no idea how far they had come but it had to be maybe 600 or so miles, due south with posse-men tracking them. Sixty more miles and they would have made it except for his partner's overwhelming anxiety about their horses.

John did not return until false-dawn and he did not come alone. He had about as scruffy a looking Indian as Tom had ever seen. Short, wiry, beady-eyed with a sweat band to hold his unwashed, long black hair. His knife sheath was empty and John had a wicked-bladed big fleshing knife stuck in his waistband. The Indian had a knot on the side of his forehead nearly the size of a goose egg. His eyes had muddy whites and, snake-like, were never still.

John pushed him to the ground, tossed the big knife aside and said, 'He didn't do it but he saw who did.'

Tom gazed at the undersized, wiry Indian. His knowledge of broncos derived from contacts hundreds of miles southward, and those were tall, stately Indians who looked straight at a man. This bird-like specimen wasn't even dressed like an Indian. He wore an old army cap with a cracked visor, a ragged, faded and unwashed butternut shirt from which the arms had been cut off to the elbows. His trousers were fringeless animal hide of some kind. Greasy, stained, but as supple as wet cloth.

There was no bead work, no feathers, no decorations at all except some crude carving on the handle of his big knife.

Ellison cheeked a cud, spat once and continued to regard the Indian, who gave an impression not of fear, but of scheming wariness.

John nudged the Indian. 'Tell him what you told me.'

To the lanky man's surprise the Indian spoke English, a guttural, not always comprehensive variety, but well enough so that most words made sense. He said, 'I heard 'em. They hid their horses, come sneakin' back here. One of 'em made a horse-sound. You two snuck out of the darkness. You went north. Them men went once around the ruin then inside. They wasn't in there long. They had some saddle-bags when they come out.'

Tom looked up. Beeson shrugged. 'Who else? Far as I can figure no one but these skulking bastards knew we was here. So who else could it be but them posse riders?'

Furnace Creek

Ellison replied dryly, 'Or them cowmen we saw yesterday.' He asked the Indian a question. 'How many was there?'

The Indian held up both hands, fingers erect except for both thumbs and both forefingers which were bent down.

John said, 'Six.'

He nudged the Indian again and nodded his head. The sinewy, dark man spoke. 'They went west aroun' the rims.'

Tom turned aside to expectorate again, then asked another question. 'You were skulkin' close by?'

The Indian shook his head vigorously. John spoke for him. 'Ghosts. I had to knock him over the head to get him this far. They're scared pee-less of these mud ruins. He tol' me they're haunted.'

Tom regarded his partner stoically. John did not meet the gaze. He had felt, and still felt, not just responsible but also humiliated. Tom had argued against leaving the saddle-bags, which held $6,000 in greenbacks from one bank robbery and one robbery of a bullion wagon with a mine payroll.

John had not mentioned it but this was to be his last robbery. He had been dreaming of settling down somewhere, maybe with a few cows, maybe with a wife, if he could find a woman willing to overlook his age, weathered look and unsmiling personality.

Tom jutted his jaw. 'What'll we do with him?'

Before the older man could answer the Indian said, 'Bones,' and touched his chest with a fist. 'I can find 'em.'

'Find who, the fellers who robbed us?'

'Yes. There ain't no place in this country I can't find

'em.'

Again Tom raised his gaze to John Beeson. The older man narrowed his eyes and barely nodded. He also spoke. 'The son of a bitch will cut our throats at the first chance, but my guess is that he can dog them thieves to a standstill. He knows the country.'

Tom jettisoned his cud, stood up and adjusted his shell belt. Before he could speak the Indian said, 'I can find 'em. They rode east. I can trail them in the night.' He also got to his feet. He firmly believed he was going to be shot if he couldn't influence the pair of larger white men, and did his utmost to negate that possibility. He even smiled at Tom Ellison.

'There ain't no better sign reader.'

Tom sighed and looked at his partner. 'Where'd you find him?'

'I didn't, the runty little rascal found me. Trouble was I went around some boulders an' when he come sneakin' along I jumped out and knocked him senseless.'

The Indian listened then addressed Tom. 'Old man plenty *coyote*.'

Tom looked stoically at the Indian. He didn't say it but he thought that if John had been *coyote*, how come they had been raided?

John said, 'He claims he can read sign in the night. Want to try him?'

Tom answered while looking at the Indian. 'He'll run off in the dark sure as I'm standin' here.'

The Indian gave Tom a proposition. 'When I get you to them men – you give me their horses.'

Tom shook his head and said, 'Let's go. If you get too far ahead I'll blow your head off.'

Furnace Creek

There was a scimitar moon which gave about the same amount of illumination as the stars. The Indian went directly where horses had been tied – and had left droppings to prove it. He did no more than briefly hesitate before moving north-westerly. Tom thought his mother must have been a bloodhound. When Tom looked at the ground he could occasionally see a shod horse imprint, but they were too few and far between to set a course by. John could have done better but he left it up to the Indian, who never slackened, not even when they came to an area of slate rock where, in daylight, it might not have been too difficult to see tracks, particularly if the horses wore calks, but the scrawny little bronco went across that rock-field like a coon dog, never faltering, never looking back.

John looked at his partner, who looked back as he said, 'We should have got the horses.'

John said nothing; once again the younger man was right.

A watery sliver of light appeared where the world ended eastward before the Indian stopped atop a slight ridge of slab-rock. He remained silent and erect for a long time before raising a skinny arm. Distantly, a thread of smoke was rising. Tom looked for buildings. There were none, the country was marginally better than it had been farther south but it seemed as devoid of two-legged life as the moon. Except for that distant spin drift of smoke rising arrow-straight into a blue void there was no sign of life.

The Indian turned toward John He would do that often. Of his two captors he preferred the older man. His reason was his own and in any case it did not matter. He said, 'They're goin' toward Stinking Spring.'

The statement meant nothing to Tom but it did to his partner. 'There's nothin' in that direction but a smell that'd gag a buzzard,' John said sceptically.

After making that statement the older man wagged his head. If the men they were pursuing continued in their present direction they would fetch up close enough to the place where hot water came out of the ground to smell it, and it was neither a pleasant place to be nor, at least in John's opinion, a destination of anyone in their right mind.

But when they began a circuitous stalk of the thin spiral of smoke it diminished until, when they were close enough, there was no smoke at all.

Tom cursed. They'd wasted several hours getting over there and, in his opinion if they hadn't spent so much time being *coyote* they probably could have caught the thieves at their breakfast fire.

But the Indian had chosen the best course. It was doubtful if his captors could have forced him to do otherwise for a simple reason, the distance from their point of sighting and the locale of the smoke was open country.

There was some consolation. From the place near the fire it was easy to pick up the trail, easier from here on because of the almost ash-like earth which took imprints very well. Now, while the men they were pursuing had too much of a head start to be visible, their sign curved around from east to north-west and John shook his head again. Within another hour or two they would catch the smell where the earth put forth hot, bad-smelling water.

Tom grumbled about all this walking and reiterated what he had said earlier: they should have got their

Furnace Creek

horses before taking up pursuit.

Neither John nor the Indian would have disputed this, but the closer they got to their destination – Stinking Spring – the more their concentration was on their destination. The Indian in particular, turned more wary by the mile. It was his nature; he did everything from life-long habit; he and his kind had been the hunted for so many years they just naturally thought and acted as the hunted.

Once when John called a halt near a stunted stand of black oaks, the Indian faced his captors and said, 'I need a gun.'

Tom answered sourly, 'When we lend you a gun it'll be a cold day in hell.'

The Indian appealed to the older man. 'I can smell Stinking Spring. That's where they went. We're close. Maybe they see us.'

John handed the bronco his carbine and warned him, 'Don't shoot no matter what until I tell you to. Understand? An' don't you face around with that gun in your hands.'

The Indian accepted the carbine and said, '*Bueno hombre*' which John understood but did not interpret, he simply motioned for the Indian to move out.

A mile farther along when the white men also caught the smell their guide faded amid some hoary rocks which were rough to the touch and too large to be movable. They followed his example, even to the point of raising their heads to peek out. What they saw made them catch their breath.

The distance was still considerable but the air was like glass. They could not make out details but one thing they had no difficulty seeing was not six men, but eight, all with horses.

Tom stared until John pulled him down out of sight. The Indian held up eight fingers and grinned. Tom saw nothing to grin about, but he was not a hunted aborigine. John got comfortable with his back to a rock, got a sliver of molasses-cured tucked into a cheek then said, 'Well now, remember them cowmen who scouted up our horses?'

Tom nodded but what bothered him was the reason six thieves might be part of a larger band with which they would have to divide the money. As an outlaw himself, he would have never met anyone, he would have chosen a different direction and kept right on riding.

This troubled the older man too, but so did something else. Whoever those men were, one thing he would have bet his life on, they were men of the law, the kind which had dogged their trail for hundreds of miles, unless of course lawmen were for sale, which was not impossible, but he had a contradictory feeling about this, and one thought that supported this feeling was that posse-riders would not know the country as well as those men at Stinking Spring evidently did.

The Indian said he would scout closer and Tom objected instantly. 'You stay with us. Understand?'

The Indian shrugged. This was the south-west where cultural lines had been blurred for centuries. Mexicans shrugged, Indians did not, but centuries of association provided Indians – whites too – with the Mexican characteristic.

John told his companions to stay where they were. Just before leaving on a scout he told Tom to watch the Indian, something he hadn't had to say, then he moved among the rocks as far northward as they remained and managed to sidle among stunted brush until he found another boulder field, which was as far as he could go.

No vegetation of any kind grew within more than a hundred yards from the place where foul-smelling water bubbled out of the earth.

He was close enough to make out details. The men nearer the watercourse were sitting on the ground with horses behind them. There seemed to be some kind of palaver in progress. If he'd had his Winchester he could have scattered those men like quail. He looked for a horse with his saddle-bags on it and did not find it; for an excellent reason, the saddle-bags were on the ground near a tall, sinewy man who was speaking to the others.

They had picked an excellent point of rendezvous. Not even itinerant travellers came near this place. Up close the odour was almost overpowering, but the men on the far side of Furnace Creek had a fair distance between them and the hot, stinking water, but it was inconceivable they would remain there long.

John crept back to his partner, settled and told them what he had seen. The Indian seemed delighted. 'Eight horses,' he said, grinning. The white men ignored him.

Tom asked if there was any way he and John could get within carbine distance and the older man shook his head. 'After sundown, maybe, but not before. The cover runs out a fair distance from where they're holdin' council.'

The Indian contradicted that. He wanted those horses very much. He had stolen other horses but not big American horses like the ones partially blocking the sight of their owners up yonder. He said, 'I can take you close, very close, if you'll do like I do.'

Tom did not question the Indian's ability to do this. What he questioned was two men and a treacherous tomahawk going up against eight men even having surprise in their favour. He said as much and John turned on him.

'They ain't goin' to set out there forever and when they leave they'll take the saddle-bags with 'em.'

The Indian made a loud grunt and pointed. From their point of vantage, unseen by the men across the creek and north-easterly, they had a perfect view of the territory to the west and what had roused the Indian made John's hair stand straight up, what there was of it.

A cloud of ash-like grey dust stood clear of the ground behind a sizeable party of riders. John made a guess and was wrong by five. He said, 'Fifteen or I'm blind.'

The Indian liked John so he did not contradict him, but he could have held up both hands fingers extended, then clenched both fists and repeated the gesture. But he didn't for an excellent reason; he was in the midst of enemies, close to thirty of them with only one man he thought might be friendly toward him, the older man who had lent the bronco his carbine.

They raised up barely enough to see the palavering horsemen across the creek and northward. They clearly had not seen the riders loping in their direction but that oversight would be corrected shortly.

John got up into a crouch, looked back, estimated the distance of the oncoming party of riders, jerked his head and led off in the direction of his earlier scout.

Neither the Indian nor Tom Ellison hesitated. They scrambled among the huge rocks as far as they could, paused to consider the riders coming from the south-west and the men across the creek, began to sidle and slither in the direction of the next jumble of prehistoric rocks.

For the Indian anything was better than sitting back there facing westerly where eventually they would have been seen. He could sneak and slither better than a lizard and made the crossing to the next field of rocks ahead of his white-skin companions, who had not lived by stealth and required more time to make the crossing.

The dust banner was noticeably closer when the three skulkers got among the boulders. John looked across the creek and sounded disgusted when he said, 'Them idiots got to be blind.'

There could have been another explanation. John's and Tom's eyes were beginning to sting from the fumes and possibly the men across the creek were having the same problem, but not for long. One of them who had been facing westerly, sprang to his feet and shouted. Instantly the entire party of eight sprang up, stood, probably in astonishment, for several seconds, then whirled, every man for himself, and struggled to get a-horseback. There was no time to snug up cinches. Two men had their saddles turn half-way and had to waste seconds pushing them back in place. They were the last pair to run for it and they had given up valuable space.

The men hiding in the rocks watched, scarcely breathing. When John expected gunfire to erupt, it didn't. He watched the large band of riders closely. However this ended it would be a horse race and the eight men's horses had been resting, the animals under their pursuers had been in a lope since they had shown their first dust banner. To an old hand like John Beeson where horseflesh had made all the difference many times, the men with his saddle-bags had a distinct advantage.

He said nothing until the large band of riders crossed the creek without even glancing in the direction of the rockfield and pushed hard in the pursuit, then John sank down and cursed. His saddle-bags were gone and being afoot there was not a chance of recovering them.

The Indian did not share John's mood until the pursuers were distant, then it struck him that the eight horses he might have had he would now never get. He sank down beside John with the carbine between his knees staring at the ground. Abruptly he leaned the Winchester aside and scuttled like a rat in several directions under the baffled gaze of the white men. He gathered every twig he could find, piled them in a pointy way atop a large rock and set them afire. He then removed his ragged, filthy old shirt and began waving it. He did this several times, kicked the twigs to scatter them and stood straight up atop the rock like a statue.

It was a long wait, the riders were small in the easterly distance. Only the dust showed prominently. The Indian finally sat atop the rock stubbornly refusing to look in any direction but the one in which he was facing It was a good long hour before he got to his feet, stood stiffly erect for several minutes, then got back down where John and Tom were sitting.

He said, 'Now comes big trouble. We go after them.'

Neither of the white men moved but John said, 'They got to be three, four miles ahead.'

The Indian did not immediately understand. To someone who was accustomed to covering distance in a mile-consuming jog because he had no horse the older white man was talking nonsense.

Tom said, 'We don't have no wings.'

The Indian finally comprehended. 'We don't have to hurry. They got my eight horses. We can catch up but we got to move.' He made a gesture of impatience and reached for the carbine. Tom blocked his arm and stood up. John also arose. He knew what the tomahawk had done and even if he'd been atop the big rock to see the very distant answering puffs of smoke he still would not have felt very encouraged, they were still afoot and everyone else was not only mounted but riding hard. John picked up the carbine and handed it to the Indian as he jerked his head for him to move out.

It was hot. Before long they would be sweating out precious water.

3
CONFUSION

An hour later, having covered a fair distance because the Indian set the pace, Tom told John one of them ought to go back for the horses. John shook his head. He told his partner the distance was too great and if one of them returned with their animals the other one and the scrawny Indian would be so far ahead they might encounter trouble.

They kept going Only once did the Indian leave his course and that was when he diverged toward an area where a solitary cottonwood tree grew. It was another boulder field. The Indian picked his way with the sure-footedness of someone who had been here before. He led them to a tiny pool of water in the heart of the rocks. There was no place to lie flat and drink and there were little vein-like paths completely surrounding the tiny spring where small animals came to this place.

They drank the tiny pool empty, had to wait for it to refill and drank again. At this place John considered the Indian carrying his Winchester and for the first time since knocking the Indian senseless, smiled at him.

Furnace Creek

As long as they did not drink perspiration was normal. As soon as they had tanked up they sweated profusely, but in a sense that was a blessing. When they continued on their way evaporation made them feel cooler.

The Indian did his best to keep them concealed. He moved between fields of rocks, underbrush which was thick in some places, and trees, which were not thick but which were not as disinclined to grow the farther east they went than they had been back in the Furnace Creek country.

They saw a small band of antelope watching them from their browsing territory. Antelope were the most curious of many deer-sized four-legged creatures. They were also among the fastest. They could out-run the fastest horse.

John saw the antelope with indifferent interest. To him the meat tasted like goat and while Mexicans and Indians liked it – and goat – John Beeson did not like either.

The Indian kept a northerly course as much as he could to avoid open country. He could not always do that but he utilized every bit of cover, even shadows, and as Tom watched he was impressed by something which the bronco had ingested with his mother's milk.

He was like a shadow, an ambulatory ghost, an intuitive natural master of stealth.

The sun climbed, the Indian never faltered, they only rested when one of the white men required it and after what seemed an eternity the Indian diverted southward from their trail and climbed atop a barren round knoll where he got belly-down and remained motionless for a long time. Both white men lay in the

Furnace Creek

same prehistoric dust, silently waiting. By now they had their complete faith in the bronco.

When he pushed up into a crouch he said, 'It will happen soon,' which, while baffling to his companions, came sooner than even the Indian expected. The sound was so distant it seemed like popping corks except for a louder, deeper sound made by old smoothbore muskets and outdated Sharps carbines.

The Indian's expression reflected inner agitation. He crouched, tense as a coiled spring gripping John's saddlegun. When he seemed about to jump and run toward the fight, Tom put a restraining hand on his arm and said, 'What'n hell's goin' on up there?'

John answered because the Indian seemed not to have heard the lanky man. 'Back yonder where he used his shirt to make smoke signals, them as saw the puffs was told of the riders comin' their way. They had plenty of time to get hid an' ready. When all them riders got close enough –'

Tom exclaimed, 'An ambush?'

John nodded and arose as the Indian did. They went down the east side of the little knob and veered northerly until they had at least a score of shod-horse tracks to follow, then followed them, only now their wiry little bronco broke over into the kind of ground-covering trot which, to him, was as natural as breathing, but which to his companions was something else.

They did not have to go the full distance, the Indian suddenly stopped, looked left and right and led off in a run toward a sit of spindly trees which provided cover only to men who got flat down. Here, he dropped, squirmed to the first tier of trees and lay like a lizard. Twice he pressed an ear to the ground. After the second time he looked over his shoulder grinning widely and said, 'Aim high. Don't shoot the horses.'

It was the large band of horsemen riding hard to get as far westward as they could. The Indian spat and said, 'Great warriors run like sheep.'

Their mounts were going up and down like sheep but not covering much ground. John said, 'Dumb sons of bitches, they'll kill them animals then where'll they be?'

Occasionally the riders swung in their saddles to look back but there was no visible pursuit, they nevertheless did not slacken up until their horses were beginning to stumble. John ground his teeth, if he could have had his way he'd have made every man-jack of those men dismount, leave their saddles and bridles behind and lead their animals on foot for as long as it took for them to get back where they'd come from. He was death on people who abused animals.

Two of the riders rode hunched forward. Tom said they had been shot, which had to be a guess but one likely to be accurate. No one rode like that unless they were ailing.

The fleeing party of riders swept past leaving only floury dust to mark their passage. When it began to diminish the Indian stood up looking eastward. There were still the other riders, the ones who had been pursued.

They did not appear. The bronco got down with one ear to the earth, arose and shook his head. He led off circling around as much as possible northerly to utilize every scrap of cover. His companions were beginning to drag their heels the way exhausted horses did. He did not allow them a moment's rest, in fact he rarely even looked back at them, his full attention was ahead. He trotted with John's carbine firmly gripped in one hand. Since his encounter with the white men he had become transformed. For one thing he'd only had that big knife before, now he had a carbine. For another thing he was an undetected pint-sized fighting man, something which never counted on size as much as it did on more valuable assets: he was on a trail and nothing else mattered.

When he finally stopped, it was because he saw several riderless horses grazing along as though nothing had happened. He counted them on both hands, then crouched forward and resumed his way being careful about sound and motion.

John came up, jerked him by the arm and scowled. 'Leave the horses be,' he exclaimed. 'That'll come later. What we want is to find the fellers who robbed our mud house back yonder. You understand?'

The Indian shook off the older man's grip, appeared about to speak then evidently changed his mind and resumed his forward movement but without trotting and without heeding the riderless horses.

Several hundred yards ahead was a flourishing stand of man-high underbrush, beyond it invisible from the west was an Indian encampment. John suspected the reason for the bronco's slackened gait and got ahead of him, moved farther north where more of that thicket curled around westerly and when the bronco would have protested John turned on him. 'Listen to me, you raggedy-assed In'ian. If you think you're goin' to lead us into your camp you're wrong.'

'Friendly,' the Indian said. 'My band is friendly.'

John's retort was short. 'Yeah, so is a nest of rattlers

Furnace Creek

until you're among 'em. Tom, keep him back with you.'

John scouted ahead angling in and out among the thorny underbrush. When he could smell dying fires he only had to cover another hundred yards and work his way southward to the fringe of the undergrowth to see the camp.

It was not very large. He did not count them but conical brush shelters with blankets thrown over their tops were scattered in a clearing. There were lazy spindrifts of smoke rising thinly from rooftop smoke-holes and near the centre of the encampment was a brush corral holding about fifteen horses and mules. The animals had nothing to eat in the corral and were lined up watching people among the brush abutments.

John had to estimate the number of Indians About fifteen, maybe twenty, it was difficult to be accurate. After the fight resulting from the ambush the Indians moved restlessly, called to one another and occasionally a buck would raise an old Sharps carbine and howl.

John went back, told Tom what he had seen and they both looked dispassionately at their bronco, who smiled disingenuously at them and said, 'Friendly – *amigos*. You understand?'

Tom settled on the ground with a thornpin bush on both sides tall enough to hide a horse. He ignored their bronco. 'From the pot into the damned fire,' he told Beeson, who did not reply until he'd cheeked a cud, then he said, 'Well, I watched them fellers they scared off an' didn't see no saddle-bags, so the other bunch and our money has go to be in the camp.'

Tom nodded about that. 'An' they know someone'll come after it, don't they?'

The Indian continued to smile and repeat that his

Furnace Creek

people were friendly, something he could not convince either of the white men was true. The broncos had ambushed and chased off a large party of riders. The others they had probably taken captive which would account for the riderless grazing horses, but the dilemma remained the same, only worse. Whether their bronco was sincere in his protestations of the friendship of his clansmen, to John Beeson who had survived his share of narrow squeaks, their Indian's assurances of safety were nothing he cared to bet his life on.

He had been down here before and although he hadn't encountered Indians he had heard stories of their stealthiness, their unwillingness to keep their word to whites and their cruel ferocity.

He took his time getting a cud in place, met the gaze of his partner and said, 'I don't trust them little bastards. They got no reason to trust us either.'

Tom nodded. 'You got any ideas?'

'Only one,' John replied. 'Stay hid until dark then see if we can sneak down there.' At his partner's expression of scepticism the older man also said, 'We got to get that money back. It's ours an' we got to get it back.'

The Indian interrupted to say, 'No white man can sneak into the camp In'ian dogs is trained to make noise when they smell whiteskins.'

John dourly eyed the Indian. 'Partner, we got to get back my saddle-bags.'

'No partner,' replied the Indian and once more struck his chest with a fist and said, 'Bones.'

John accepted that. 'All right, Bones. We're goin' to get our money back, dogs be damned. If your people get roiled up we'll kill as many as we can.'

Furnace Creek

'They will kill you,' Bones replied.

John nodded. 'Maybe. Let me explain something to you, Bones. I'm getting old. Them saddle-bags got the money that'll make it likely for me to go somewhere an' settle down in my old age. You understand? Hell, I might as well get killed yonder because I can't no longer raid for money.'

Tom gazed steadily at his partner who, in fact, had chosen this way of explaining that he was not going raiding any more, but John and the Indian ignored the lanky man and regarded only each other for a long time before the Indian spoke.

'I will go to camp. You stay here. I will find if they have the saddle-bags and come back to tell you.'

'Likely,' Tom said dryly. 'You'll come back with a herd of stronghearts.'

The Indian, who had never cared for Tom Ellison, flared out at him. 'You can set here. The In'ians will find you. Then where will you be?' He jutted his chin in John's direction and spoke in border Mexican. '*Bueno hombre.*' He held up John's carbine to emphasize what he had said and spoke next in English. 'You would have shot me back at the haunted place. This man let me have a gun.'

Tom understood. He also understood something else. Captive tomahawks were about as reliable as peccaries and were just as fierce.

Tom looked at his partner. 'Let's wait for dark,' he said, and leaned his Winchester against the springy branches of a thornpin bush, eased back and tipped his hat over both eyes. As far as he was concerned that ended the discussion.

In fact it did end it. John shrugged, considered

Bones and said, 'You can't blame him. He's heard about treacherous In'ians, an' I like the notion of waitin' until they're asleep down there an' –'

'They won't all be asleep,' Bones replied. 'An' the dogs never sleep.' For the first time he used the older man's name. He said, 'We come this far for your paper money an' my horses. We done well together. John, you can trust me.'

John never knew whether he could or not. From the corner of his eye he saw a bare brown arm reach through the thicket where Tom had leaned his carbine and without a sound grasp the weapon and very carefully take it from sight without so much as making a single thornpin branch quiver.

John did not move except for his face, he turned back toward Bones, who was looking straight back as impassive as stone when he said, 'I told you they would find you. We never sleep without scouts out in all directions. If whites from the towns don't hunt us for sport, the Messicans come up from the south an' hunt us because they hate In'ians. An' the army hunts us because it is their job. We never sleep for long in one place. We never sleep well at all, even with scouts watching for sign.'

John continued to look at the Indian. 'How many?' he said.

Bones held up both hands fingers extended, closed both fists and displayed the same gesture again.

'An' they're around us in the brush?'

'Yes. If you touch your gun in the holster they will shoot an' you will not see anyone to shoot back at.'

John spat his cud aside, all the sweetness had been leached out. He looked at his sleeping partner and

Furnace Creek

back to the Indian. 'Did you somehow tell them about us?'

Bones shook his head. 'No. There was no way to. But them riders they ambushed liked to have kicked a hornets' nest. The people now have to move quick. John, you're a good man. I told you what I would do an' you give me eight horses. You make honest trade an' so do I.'

Bones straightened up to call out but John stopped him with a gesture. He knew how Tom Ellison acted when abruptly aroused in danger. John leaned, gently shook the lanky man until Tom used one hand to push the hat off his face and look annoyedly at his partner. John said, 'Lie where you are. Don't even look like you want to pull your Colt.'

Tom's eyes steadily widened. He saw Bones regarding him from an expressionless face and lurched to get hoisted on one elbow.

John kept his grip on the younger man's arm as he spoke again. 'They got your carbine an' they're all around us hid in the brush.'

Tom swung his head but the carbine was not there, he swung it back and glared at Bones, 'I knew he'd trick us some way, the son of a bitch.'

John continued to speak quietly. 'He didn't trick us. He's all we got to stay alive.'

'If he he didn't trick us how come they got us surrounded?'

'What'd you expect after them riders dang near come into their camp an' got bushwhacked? They're roiled up same as you'd be. They had scouts out. Findin' us wasn't hard, for folks like they are.'

Tom sat up, pulled his hat far enough to keep the

sunlight from reaching his eyes and very methodically looked in both directions then back where his saddle-gun had been. There was nothing but the absence of the gun to indicate there were Indians watching their every move. He blew out a big breath and spoke to their bronco.

For a long time they looked at each other before Tom said, 'All right. We got bushwhacked too, but I can tell you without even our horses you won't get much off us.'

Bones slowly arose holding John's Winchester. He gestured for them to also stand up, which they did. Bones then scarcely raised his voice as he said something guttural and completely incomprehensible to the white men.

The first Indian came from the manzanita behind John and Tom. He was holding Tom's Winchester. Other Indians seemed to barely move the thicket as they came through it. In all there were nine of them, mostly older men but with several bucks about the age of Bones.

They were thin and ragged and the whites of their eyes were muddy, but every man among them had a sheath knife and a carbine. One older man also had a big old horse pistol in a holster that had US stamped on it. Bones addressed John. 'Drop your pistols,' which both white men did, then Bones addressed the old bronco with the hawgleg in the US holster.

The old man listened, did not say a word but gestured for Bones to lead the way to the camp through the thicket.

4
A CHANGE IN PLANS

The band was small, the people weathered dark and wary-eyed. There were men armed with a variety of old weapons: about the only thing each man carried which hadn't changed over the centuries was a sheath knife.

Bony dogs met the party of broncos with their white captives by darting to bite and snarl until they were shouted at then they slunk away.

The women were mostly small and lean. John and Tom did not see a fat Indian in the camp, nor did they see any who were other than ragged and half wild.

The white men were herded toward a smouldering fire pit and pushed to the ground. Among the dark, muddy-eyed men who sat around them there were several who showed more curiosity than hostility.

Bones spoke at some length and twice pointed to John Beeson. Whatever he had said seemed not to have made much impression. At least the Indians showed nothing in their expressions.

One old man, lined and bony, spoke shortly and Bones held aloft John's Winchester as he launched into another oration to which the Indians gravely listened without any change of expression.

A youngish Indian addressed John. Their custom was to consider older men first. He spoke in Spanish, but soon switched to English because of the blank look on the faces of the captives.

His English was no better than that of Bones but it was understandable. He wanted to know why the captives were in the Furnace Creek country.

John answered forthrightly. 'We were going to Mexico, or some other place.'

The Indian said, 'Why?'

John replied looking the Indian in the eye, 'I've been down here before a couple of times, but not for long.'

'Why now?' the Indian repeated.

John briefly hung fire before saying, 'We took some money.'

'Stole it? You are outlaws?'

John nodded bleakly.

The Indians spoke among themselves, ignoring the white men and Bones, who sat down next to John and mumbled, 'They like what you said.'

When the discussion concluded among the Indians that same stringy-hided old man looked at John but addressed Bones. After the old man stopped speaking Bones interpreted to Ellison and Beeson. 'Enemy of white men is friend of Indian,' he said, looking relieved. 'The spokesman wants to know if you can get good guns for us?'

John had to think for a moment. This was something Beeson had not expected. He looked at Bones, read the anticipation correctly and replied. 'I don't know this country that well. I got no idea where there are guns.'

Bones did not interpret, he replied to John briskly, 'We know the country. We know every town, every ranch. We know the stores that sell guns.'

John scowled faintly. 'They'd be expensive, Bones.'

Bones addressed the spokesman, who replied curtly and one of the younger braves left the fire ring. John and Tom accepted the sudden silence. Even Bones, sitting with them, said nothing.

The surprise of both Beeson and Ellison was complete when the Indian returned and dropped a pair of saddle-bags at the feet of the spokesman, who methodically unbuckled one side, raised the flap and tilted the saddle-bag so that John and Tom could see its contents. Their money.

The old man watched the captives with unblinking snake-like eyes before rebuckling the flap and saying, 'Plenty money', in English.

John's gaze drifted to the smouldering coals and remained there until Bones nudged him and muttered, 'He wants you to use the money to get good guns.'

For the first time Tom spoke and looked directly at the old Indian as he did so. 'Where are the sons of bitches who stole the money from us?'

Bones interpreted, listened to the answer and interpreted again. 'Tied in a hogan.'

'All of 'em?'

Again the old man spoke and was interpreted. 'No,' Bones said and held up one hand with three bent fingers.

John nodded. 'Three got killed?'

Bones nodded. He and the spokesman then spoke back and forth at length, during which time John got a cud settled in his cheek, expectorated into the smouldering fire-pit and several Indians laughed but the old man was not one of them. He pointed a gnarled finger at John and spoke in English. 'You buy guns. You buy bullets. You live.'

Tom settled more comfortably on the ground but remained silent. Bones looked at the older white man from an expressionless face as he said, 'I told him you give me carbine. I said you are a good white man. I told him you will help us.'

John muttered aside, 'Thanks. Don't do me no more favours', and returned his attention to the spokesman. 'My name is John.'

The old man nodded. *'Juan.* My name is Mexican Horse.' He then spoke in Mex Spanish until John rolled his eyes, then the old man used his own dialect to Bones, who addressed John in English. 'He said, great wealth in saddle-bags. You buy guns and still have much left.'

John looked pained. 'Tell him, Bones, that good guns cost much money. Too much for what's in the saddle-bags.'

The old man listened attentively then sent another Indian toward one of the hogans. Tom leaned and whispered to Beeson, 'Old bastard's got money.'

But it wasn't money the bronco returned with, it was two Mex *alforas* which held jewellery including several magnificent large golden crucifixes. There were inlaid Chihuahua spurs and bridles also rings of gold, some with inset brilliant stones.

Beeson and Ellison looked in awe until Bones said, 'From raids into Messico. But we can't sell em an' don't wear them. You can sell them.'

John was shaking his head until the spokesman said

Furnace Creek

something brusquely for Bones to interpret. 'He wants to know why your partner shakes his head.'

Tom looked at the old Indian while replying in English. 'Mister, if we tried to sell this stuff the law'd be on us like a rash.' Tom gestured toward the hoard. 'That's plunder. Anyone trying to peddle that stuff in Messico would end up in front of a firing squad. Up here it wouldn't be much different.'

John gravely nodded in agreement. The old Indian sat gazing at the captives a long time, until a younger man leaned and mumbled gutturally to him, then the old man addressed John again.

'You buy it from your saddle-bags. We sell it to you. You get it cheap. Then we give you back money and you buy guns.'

John gazed pensively at the spokesman. Clearly the old devil spoke and understood English. All the business of using an interpreter was for effect. John spoke directly to the old man. 'What could we do with this junk?'

'Sell it,' the old man retorted. 'Make much money.'

John sighed. For a long time there was no more said. Several women came to the fire-pit with what appeared to be *quesdillas*, folded over tacos but much smaller. They left them on a large wooden platter and departed without speaking or raising their eyes.

Bones reached for food and while eating, said, 'John you do what the spokesman says.' He swallowed before saying the rest of it. 'Or they kill you like they're goin' to do with them others in the hogan.'

The Indians ate, ignored the white men and talked among themselves. Interruptions, even curses, were clearly evident.

When John finished his third *quesdilla* and had wiped his hands down the outside of each trouser leg he spoke to the old man again. 'What towns got guns an' where are they?'

The old man swallowed before replying, this time in his own language so Bones interpreted. 'He said we will show you, but only from a distance. He say we surround the town from far out and hide, an' if you try to run away or if the people in them towns come boilin' out we'll know you told them, an' we will kill you an' as many of them as we can.'

John picked his teeth: whatever meat had been in those little sandwiches had been stringy and full of sinews. He did not want to dwell on what the meat was but suspected it had been lizard or snake. The old Indian used a ragged shirt-tail to wipe grease from his face and said, 'You take plunder far away an' sell it.'

John considered that. It was possible, but he and Tom would have to travel a very great distance to do it. The spokesman took John's pensive silence as agreement and mightily belched before speaking again, this time for Bones to interpret. He told John he had been told there was many times over the value in the *alforjas* for what was in John's saddle-bags, and again Beeson grew thoughtful.

The old man was probably right, but that was not the difficulty. There was no place west of the Missouri River where people would not know just by looking that the plunder had been stolen. In the east they might not guess that, or might not care, but John had never been east of the river.

Tom leaned to whisper, 'Ask the old goat if we can talk to the men they got tied up.'

Bones interpreted and the spokesman's reply was harsh. Bones addressed the partners. 'He say no. He say he want answer now. Will you get us guns or not.' Then Bones added something the old man had not said. 'Get guns. They will kill you before sunset.'

John leaned, pulled the *alforjas* closer and looked inside, even ran his fingers through the plunder. Not a word was said and not an eye left him until he leaned back nodding. Then several broncos smiled and the old man said to Bones the captives could talk to the other prisoners and told Bones which brush shelter they were in. He then arose to depart and the other Indians followed him, except for one with a knife scar from one cheek to the other and an indentation where the blade had cut deepest across his nose.

This man never left them. He ignored Bones and did not utter a word. He carried one of those old shot-out Sharps guns and a big fleshing knife in a belt sheath.

Aside from the face scar this Indian, who was very dark, and was probably at least half Mexican, had one other unique characteristic: he wore Mexican shoes with huge-roweled Chihuahua spurs attached. The spurs were musical when he walked because the rowels dragged in the dust. His name was, appropriately, Scar, but neither John nor Tom would know that for some time.

The hogan where five prisoners sweated profusely with hands held tightly behind their back by thongs and whose ankles were similarly bound, looked more than just demoralized, they stared at Tom and John, Bones and the scar-faced man from eyes made dull from equal parts of demoralization and thirst.

John told Bones they needed water. Bones told Scar

who remained rooted as though he were deaf. Bones then went after water.

John and Tom hunkered in silence gazing at the bound captives. One said, 'I know you. You in cahoots with these flea-bag renegades?'

Before speaking John looked around but Scar showed nothing on his face.

'They caught us in some underbrush,' John told the beard-stubbled, unwashed men. 'We seen you meet with some other fellers at that stinkin' spring. Where are they?'

The answer came from a greying man with sunk-set grey eyes. 'Dead. They let us go past then run us down on fresher horses. We fought but they used knives. '

'Who are you?' Tom asked, and got a sour look from one of the bound men. 'Hired riders.'

'Who hired you?'

'The law up north. Hired us to find you two an' fetch back the money you stole.'

John arose because one knee was bothering him – the left one. He asked one of the bound men, a stocky individual with grey at the temples if he could imitate a nickering horse. Instead of replying the man threw back his head and duplicated a horse very convincingly. Afterwards he said, 'Learnt it from the Crow. The best horse stealers in the country.'

The man beside him said, 'It worked, you went lookin' for your horses.'

John took time to bite a corner off his plug, which the stocky greying man watched with interest before he said, 'Couldn't share a cud could you?'

John bent, held the plug until the bound man cheeked it then arose pocketing the tobacco. He waited until the greying man had settled the chew then asked him another question. 'Who was that bunch that chased you an' got bushwhacked by the In'ians?'

The greying man answered candidly, 'Damned if I know. But all of a sudden they came at us an' we run.'

'Why?' Tom asked.

The greying man put a disgusted look at Ellison before replying, 'What would you have done? We had saddle-bags full of greenbacks an' whoever they was they was armed to the teeth chargin' straight at us A big mob of 'em. Didn't take much sense to see we was outnumbered to hell an' back an' they wasn't friendly.'

The greying man paused as though in recollection then spoke again. 'I'll tell you one thing, mister, them gents give us a hell of a chase. If they hadn't been ridin' wore-down horses they'd have got close enough to shoot us like pigeons on a roost. I got no idea who they was, but they sure as hell bent on catchin' us for a fact.'

Bones returned with one US canteen which did not hold much water, and two long pouches made of antelope intestines full of water. It would have been a good guess that normally the bound men would have refused the water bags but not now, They drained the bags and the canteen. Instantly fresh sweat burst out over them. They could do nothing but narrow their eyes and shake their heads to avoid having sweat in their eyes.

The greying man studied John briefly then asked a question. 'You follered us?'

Tom dryly replied, 'On foot.'

The greying man's eyes widened. 'On foot? You lose your horses?'

John ignored the question. He was worrying about

that big band of riders the Indians had routed. 'That was quite a bunch that chased you,' he said and the greying man agreed. 'Must've been half the cowmen in the country.'

John frowned faintly. 'Cowmen?'

'Cowmen, mister. Every man-jack of 'em had lass ropes on their saddles.'

An Indian came to the opening, said something to Bones which the scar-faced men implemented by jerking his old carbine in the direction of the door hole.

They went outside and stopped in their tracks. Indians were hurrying every which way, filling *alforjas*, sacks, even rolls of bedding. Children were holding horses and mules. The Indians ignored the men in front of the hogan and called back and forth. John said 'Strikin' camp.'

Bones agreed. 'Mexican Horse said to when we was at the fire-pit.'

Tom raised his eyebrows. 'Mexican Horse? The old man's spokesman?'

Bones nodded while watching what seemed to be organized chaos. 'I got to find my eight horses,' he said, and left Tom and John with the stone-faced scarred Indian, who seemed less interested in the hasty preparations for moving than he was in the prisoners.

Tom tried to address him by asking where the people would go. Scar looked Tom directly in the eyes and did not speak.

A bird-like old woman, grey as a badger with her hair braided in back paused with an armload and spoke in English to John Beeson. 'You son bitch bring trouble,' she said, and marched away, her back as straight as a ramrod. Scar faintly smiled but his prisoners did not

Furnace Creek

notice.

Bones and a large man got into an argument over three of the saddled horses. The large Indian knocked Bones down. As he sprang up he reached for his knife. The sheath was empty. The big buck cursed Bones in Spanish and jerked on the shanks to lead the horses away.

Bones jumped on the large Indian's back, tried to get the man's knife. The larger Indian snarled, flung Bones off and kicked him hard.

Tom let out a roar and ran at the big Indian. As the bronco turned, surprised, Tom hit him on the slant of the jaw. He went down in a heap.

Within moments a dozen Indians surrounded Tom. Bones got to his feet talking excitedly. John started forward and Scar jammed him over the kidneys from behind with his carbine barrel and growled something incomprehensible to the white man, but the blow from behind made John stop and lock his jaw in pain.

The old spokesman came out, angrily told the Indians to go back to work, and as they drifted away he addressed Bones, who interpreted for Tom. 'He said for them to leave you alone. He told them you are worth much more alive than dead.'

The old spokesman stamped away, still angry.

The large Indian was regaining consciousness. He tried to rise. Tom caught one arm and helped him up. there was a flung-back, thin trickle of blood on the right side of the Indian's mouth. He stood a long time staring straight at Tom. From some distance the old man known as Mexican Horse, shrilled loudly. The big bronco walked away trailing the lead ropes to three horses on the ground.

Furnace Creek

As Bones retrieved the ropes he said. '*Bueno hombre*,' and left Tom standing there. It was over but the Indians eyed Tom askance as they worked. The Indian was one of their most formidable warriors.

Tom went back to John whose back was still painful and Scar back-peddled far enough to be out of Tom's reach. He held his old gun low in both hands with a thumb on the hammer. Tom ignored him as John said, 'I thought you didn't like Bones?'

'I don't but that other buck was ten inches taller and heavier. I never liked bullies.'

'You could've got yourself killed.'

Tom ignored that to say, 'Where are they goin'?'

John said, 'Ask 'em. I don't know.'

Tom turned to face Scar whose thumb tightened on the gun hammer and repeated the question. 'Where are they goin'?'

Scar, obviously a tough fighting man himself, answered in English, which surprised John so much he also faced around.

Scar said, 'Messico.'

Tom let go a long breath. 'Why? Because some damned cowmen got shot at?'

Scar's answer was cryptic and again in English. 'Cowmen come back with soldiers.'

Tom faced back around looking at John, who had something to say but not when the broncos behind him understood English, so he just shrugged.

5
WATER

Indians on the move did so without order. Old women with willow switches herded children and dogs with sticks. The men rode, for the most part silent and wary. When the straggling cavalcade had to cross open country, which it did often, outriders left the band in all directions. Tom and John rode two of those saddled animals that had belonged to the prisoners in the hogan; they, in turn walked with a woman on each side who was astride and had a rawhide rope from the saddlehorn to a wrist of each prisoner.

Bones rode up ahead with Mexican Horse. Other men were scattered among the pack animals, dogs, mounted women and walking Indians.

The sun was high and would not appreciably cool even after it sank in the west.

Inevitably dust rose and lingered in a breathless day. Tom was stoic. His partner was thoughtful. Among the baggage somewhere were the saddle-bags and that *alforja* loaded with stolen plunder.

They stopped just short of sundown at a watering place where the horses were turned out to browse under the watchful care of youngsters.

A fire was made of red-barked manzanita which burned so hot and fiercely only the toughest old women dared get close. There was an advantage, manzanita made practically no smoke.

John and Tom, in the company of stoic, hawk-eyed Scar, went to the water-hole. After drinking, Mexican Horse motioned for them to be seated. It appeared to be the custom for the men to gather in one place while the women made a meal, scolded children, threw stones at hungry dogs and gabbled among themselves like geese.

Other Indians were colourful; these were not. They wore almost no jewelry, feathers or beadwork. They were purely and simply raiders concerned with plundering in a territory where every hand was against them. They struggled, deceived, hid, stole, fled, fought and moved often. As Tom told John on the ride to the water-hole they were the most miserable creatures he had ever seen. John gently smiled as he replied, 'Every man has a country. In this country that's how folks survive. It's steal beef when there's no game, shoot trespassers, never stay long in one place. It's a hell of an existence but they likely wouldn't last long any other place.'

Mexican Horse had been thoughtful on the ride. He told Bones he wanted to talk to John, and when the white man came forward he and the old bronco sat on the ground with Mexican Horse stating what he had been thinking when he said, 'In Messico they got poor guns. The ammunition makes big smoke an' the bullets don't go far.'

John listened attentively. The old buzzard hadn't

Furnace Creek

needed an interpreter. John sat there watching a large black ant. Out of nowhere a pink tongue moved with lightning speed and the ant disappeared. John had to look closely to see the lizard. It blended perfectly with its surroundings. If it was motionless it would be almost invisible.

Mexican Horse used Bones to interpret. Obviously he was more comfortable in his own language. Bones on the other hand seemed proud of his English, which was bad but understandable. He interpreted what the old man had said. 'He says you can ride anywhere. Your only enemy is age. He say he is old and can't help it. Can't ride anywhere. Too many enemies.'

John smiled at the lizard. The old man was rough and tough and shrewd. John looked at the lean, lined, old weathered face and for a moment felt – not sympathy – kinship. He addressed Bones, sure the spokesman would understand.

'He isn't old, he is tired.'

Bones interpreted and the old man put a steady gaze on John. He was tired, but that was because he was old. When he had been young he was never tired. He brought the subject to guns by saying, 'You can ride to the towns. We can show you where they are.'

John sighed soundlessly. He couldn't ride freely; he also had enemies, maybe mostly on paper tacked to buildings with one word in bold black letters : WANTED, and in small letters DEAD OR ALIVE.

Again Bones interpreted. 'Mexican Horse say you go an' Tom stay.'

John shook his head, not in disagreement but because the half wild old man who couldn't read or write, was smart without those advantages. He looked again at the old man, spoke directly to him. 'I got reasons for wantin' to avoid towns, but most of all I got trouble with what you want, guns to kill people.'

The old man's reply came without hesitation, and again Bones had to put it into English. 'He say our clan used to be many numbers. We been hunted, shot, trapped, even poisoned like coyotes.'

John scratched inside his shirt, looked over where horse and household equipment was scattered indiscriminately and spoke without looking at either Indian.

'I don't want your plunder. I couldn't sell it. You give me money an' I'll buy guns. But you tell Mexican Horse me'n my partner are outlaws bein' hunted. We might get caught in one of those towns.'

The old man's answer to that was brief. 'If they catch you we turn your friend loose.'

John looked for the lizard but it was gone. He said, 'Bones, tell him if I get guns his bucks will carry war to ranches an' settlements.'

The old man's answer to that was again brief. 'He say no, we go live in Messico. It would be better for us down there. More In'ians, bigger mountains, better grass and water. We have to leave Furnace Creek country. He say soldiers right now huntin' us.'

John looked quickly at the old Indian, who nodded his head. 'They come,' he said in English. 'We see their dust, their scouts, the night fires.'

Even Bones had been surprised. He spoke rapidly and the old man answered the same way. John had to wait but eventually Bones said, 'Scouts see them yesterday. Soldiers an' them cowmen we ran off. Scouts waited until late night then tried to stampede their horses. No good. They got steel hobbles an' locks an' too many soldiers watching horses.'

John said, 'How far?'

The old man answered by raising one skinny arm pointing north-westward. 'One day.'

John's heart sank. The horses and pack mules of Mexican Horse's band had never been properly cared for. Stockmen and soldiers did not ride poor animals. He squinted northwesterly as he said, 'How far to Messico?'

Bones answered, 'Two more days.'

John spoke directly to Mexican Horse. 'It is too late for men to get guns for you. It will be too late for everything unless you make better time, an' even then you're leavin' tracks a child could follow.'

The old man grinned. 'If they catch us they will kill you too. White man with Indians no good.'

Tom came over with Scar ten feet behind him. He sat down, nodded and listened to every word his partner said with widening eyes. When John had finished Tom said, 'What we doin' settin' here?' and stood up.

Mexican Horse also arose, but with some difficulty. He said, 'We want guns.'

Tom exploded. 'You crazy old screwt, you got the army breathin' down your neck. Even if you had good guns, leavin' tracks like you're doin' they'd be all over you like chicken pox.'

Before Bones could interpret John spoke up. 'If the army an' some hang-rope cowmen catch you'n me with the Indians –'

He got no chance to finish it. A woman began trilling. The men near the spring looked back. An Indian on a nearly wind-broke horse slid off the animal and kept right on sliding until he was crumpled in the dirt. That old woman with the braided hair shrieked and ran forward. The Indian was her son, her only son.

Mexican Horse went where the young bronco was lying. Gruffly he told some men to care for the horse then stood looking down at the woman who was holding her son's head on her arms as she rocked and moaned.

John leaned close to Mexican Horse and said, 'Dead.'

The old man neither acknowledged the crowd nor the kneeling woman. He opened the bloody shirt, looked briefly at the wound and straightened up. The youth had been shot through the body. It was a wonder he'd been able to reach the camp.

Bones tugged at John's sleeve. When they were away from the crowd Bones said, 'She is sister to Mexican Horse. Her boy was the only one left of his family.'

Three broncos got mounted and struck out on the dead youth's back trail. Each one carried a carbine. Mexican Horse went with his sister to a quiet place among the sandstone boulders. They placed the youth with his head facing east and soundlessly began piling rocks atop him. The woman had tears streaming but never made a sound nor slackened in her work of piling rocks. Old Mexican Horse looked bitter and grim. The world was slowly overtaking his tribesmen and himself like a grindstone.

John sought Tom to make a statement. 'He rode the horse hard. I'd say someone shot him maybe an hour before. No more'n that or he wouldn't have made it. You know what that means?'

Tom knew. 'They're close behind us.'

John nodded. 'Someone is.'

Most of the afternoon was gone before the straggling

Indians were again under way. Now, even the children and dogs were quiet.

When the men who had ridden back returned they went directly to the front where Mexican Horse was stoically riding. He did an odd thing, to his tribesmen anyway, he twisted and beckoned John to ride stirrup with him and the men who had reported on their scout.

The old man abandoned the pride which had prevented him from speaking English. He said, 'Juan, it is the men we ambushed, but many more.'

John had expected worse. 'No soldiers?'

'Far back,' the old man replied.

'How far back?'

Mexican Horse spoke aside briefly with one of the scouts, then said, 'One day back.'

John, who had worried about soldiers had no heart for a fight with the army, but cowmen . . . he smiled at the old man. 'Too many cowmen?'

The old man answered curtly. 'For us too many. Maybe thirty, forty.'

John squinted ahead where heat waves danced. 'Any water up ahead?'

Mexican Horse nodded, then quickly looked at Beeson, who smiled without speaking. Mexican Horse gave an order to his scouts who turned back to go among the straggling, sweating mob yelling for haste.

Mexican Horse looked at John and made a fist of his right hand and struck the area of his heart with it. John was not familiar with the gesture but made a guess and said, 'I didn't pick this mess an' maybe you didn't neither, but those bastards back yonder wouldn't believe us, they'd shoot first, so we got to get to the water first.'

Furnace Creek

Mexican Horse sat straighter on his horse. John dropped back to explain to Tom what he had done. Behind Tom, Scar, expressionless as always, stared at the older white man without showing anything on his face, and kept staring.

John turned to ask Scar if the water they were heading for was the only source of water and the burly Indian answered in Spanish. One word. '*Si.*'

The sun was a malevolent pale disc overhead. Heat waves hindered distant visibility. Most of the people and all of the animals were suffering. When the scouts used quirts to make the animals move the best they could do was a shambling trot.

The people on foot had water bags, the animals had no water.

John hoped very hard the water they were heading for was not far. If it was they were going to lose animals.

Behind them Scar anticipated John's anxiety and this time he spoke two words in Spanish. '*Dos varas.*'

Tom turned testily and yelled at Bones who was back with the woman who had lost her son. Bones came up and Tom repeated the two Spanish words. Bones answered in English, 'About two, three miles.' He also asked how close the soldiers were and Tom irritably explained it wasn't soldiers it was cowmen the Indians had bushwhacked, that the soldiers were a day's ride farther back.

Bones dropped back to explain why they were hurrying and who was chasing them.

They raised considerable dust which, normally, their pursuers would see but the sun was blindingly bright, the dust was pale. For once dust did not worry John nor his partner.

When Mexican Horse began veering south-westerly toward one of those prehistoric jumbles of huge colourless rocks, John's anxiety lessened.

The spring of warm water was in the centre of a large, brushy clearing. Tom was impressed. 'Rocks all around,' he told his partner.

The animals were drooping badly. Mexican Horse gave orders that packs and saddles were to be removed. He then stationed a dozen men around the reservoir of water to prevent the animals from foundering themselves, which was no simple task. They had to use whips. A horse or mule in the last stages of thirst drank too much, which was understandable, but the results often was chest-founder. The Indians kept the animals from tanking up except after long intervals and taking a little water after each interval.

The turmoil was pure chaos. The clearing barely held the people and animals. Indians guarded every separation of rocks so the animals could not leave. The people had to fill their gut pouches and their stomachs with muddied water, but that mattered less than what they drank was wet.

John looked for their shadow. Bones told them Scar had gone to scout with other broncos. John had no time to speculate why the Indian who had dogged them had suddenly left.

Several old people collapsed and were rigged with shelter from the sun. John and Tom used their hats to dip water and wash the backs of their animals. Bones, whose solitary motivating thought for days was eight horses, watched then led his mount up to also wash its back.

Furnace Creek

Tom climbed atop a huge, high, rough-sided rock and looked back. He could not make out dust. When he climbed down the Indians were eating. Bones brought some twisted, bone-dry jerky that had been cured with more pepper than salt, handed it to the white men and said, 'There is another place of water,' and used his arm to point westward. 'Seven miles. Poison water.' As Bones lowered his arm he grinned.

Mexican Horse came over and squatted. He seemed impervious to the heat and the burning sun. He chewed for a moment and swallowed before speaking. He surprised both John and Tom by speaking Spanish. Neither of them had thought the old man even spoke English six hours before. Bones interpreted. 'Mexican Horse say you belong with us. He say you go down into Messico with us, live safe down there. We know the Chiricahuas better than the Messicans.' Bones made an expansive gesture. 'Big. Chiricahuas big mountains. Apaches lived down there for many lifetimes. Messicans are afraid to go into those places.'

John replied dryly, 'One thing at a time. We're a helluva way from bein' home free.'

Mexican Horse left them to go among the people. He sat in boulder-shade with his sister without either of them saying a word.

The animals had only wiry bushes to eat. There had never been grass in this place, not even around the water-hole. John speculated that if they could slip away after dark they just might get into Mexico before the soldiers came up. If they couldn't, he had no doubt at all about how this was going to end, but although he and Tom talked neither of them mentioned their fears to the Indians.

Scar returned with his old carbine in the crook of one arm, took his place close to the white men, out of reach but close, and sat like a dark, sweaty Buddha.

That big Indian Tom had knocked unconscious joined them. He and Scar grunted through a brief guttural discussion then the big bronco departed without even glancing at the white men.

Scar said, 'Getting close.' He and Bones talked at some length before Bones interpreted. Midway through he was interrupted by Tom who jerked a thumb in Scar's direction and asked why he didn't talk directly to them.

Bones squirmed. He could not explain because Scar was sitting there and would understand every word, so he simply said. 'Speak Mex an' our language. No English.'

Tom leaned to say this was not true when John caught him by the arm, hard. 'Leave it be,' he warned Ellison. 'It ain't important. What is – how far is the border from here?'

Bones answered. 'Six, eight miles.'

John sighed in silence, That was a great distance to worn out horses and mules. Scar arose, walked away and after his departure Bones spoke quietly. 'White people hanged his father an' brother. He hates everything to do with whites.'

An old man brought them a gut water bag. It was muddy tasting. They drank, handed back the shrunken pouch but the old man did not leave. He said something which Bones interpreted. 'He say Messicans keep him in prison four years. Two white men got him out in the night.'

Tom sighed. 'Great country you picked, John. Even

the damned bugs can kill you if the water don't.'

Scar returned, sat stoically as before with his old gun slanted across one arm. He looked straight ahead into the diminishing pandemonium.

Now that they were watered and rested, the Indians ate, gabbled among themselves, ignored the white men and once or twice there was laughter.

John watched and listened and wondered if these Indians hadn't lived their bare-bones, dangerous existence so long any respite, even one under these conditions, was genuinely pleasurable to them.

Scar leaned and spoke gutturally to Bones, whose eyes widened. He did not interpret for a long moment, then all he said was, 'They know where we are. They are out there.'

John squinted skyward. The sun was descending, getting redder by the moment as it passed through earth's dust.

Tom arose to walk through the little camps to some large rocks. He climbed the largest one. An Indian already up there gestured for Tom to lie flat.

What he saw was daunting. Their pursuers which Bones had estimated at roughly thirty looked to Tom more like fifty or sixty, and every one of them was armed to the gills.

They were staying out of gun range, palavering, occasionally staring at the boulder field. The prone Indian said, 'No water.'

Tom climbed back down, went where John was and told the older man what he had seen. He also added a little more. 'If the soldiers make a forced march they'll be here come sunup.'

There was a slight commotion, the five prisoners

Furnace Creek

cursed some Indians because they hadn't got as much water as they needed. This outburst was remedied by the old spokesman. He told some bucks to take the captives to the water-hole, let them drink their fill then hold their heads under water to make sure they got enough water to keep them quiet for a while.

6
DIMINISHING OPPORTUNITIES

The posse-riders gathered brush and made a fire. By its light watchers could see men moving. Bones told Tom their enemies would camp by their fire, which made Tom hunt his partner and suggest the Indians wait until midnight then sneak away.

John took this idea to Mexican Horse. The old man listened, nodded and walked away without agreeing or disagreeing. In fact he and several warriors had decided on this course an hour before Tom suggested it, but the camp continued to be disorganized. In fact the old people rolled into thin blankets and slept.

John worried about the animals. He told Bones they were too tuckered up to make the final dash with packs and riders.

Mexican Horse came to John after Tom went back to lie atop the big rock to watch the distant camp and its ghost-like shadows.

The old man had been through sieges before. He told John if they abandoned the animals their enemies could overtake them on horseback before they reached the border. He looked both downcast and tired.

Furnace Creek

John asked the old man if he had friends among other tribes in the area. Mexican Horse shook his head as he answered. Not many. Some Apaches, but they were already in the Chiricahuas.

John cheeked a fresh chew, sat gazing past the old man at the ragged, chaotic camp and said, 'Horses won't last. They been hungry too long.'

Mexican Horse stared back. 'They don't take *prisoneros*. We are vermin to them. Even the very young. *Comprendo?*'

John squinted into the failing daylight at the old man. 'One thing left.' He struggled to remember the Spanish word. He'd picked up a smattering of Spanish years ago in his earlier trip to the South Desert country. 'One thing left, *viejo*.'

'*Que?*'

John was annoyed. '*Que* what?'

'*Que* means what.'

John stifled a profane comment. These damned people and their interchangeable language! 'Talk to them.'

Mexican Horse's eyes narrowed. 'They don't talk they shoot,' he said.

John persisted. 'There ain't anything left to do. Maybe talkin' will stop a massacre.'

'No. They came here to kill us. For them to get it over with. Talk – no good.' Mexican Horse brightened. 'You talk, we sneak away. Maybe get far enough.'

John was surprised. The old warrior should have known better. 'They'll have these rocks surrounded. A snake couldn't sneak away.'

Scar appeared out of the descending dusk to speak curtly and depart. He did not look at John.

Mexican Horse said, 'All around the rocks.'

John nodded, he was not surprised. 'Talk, that's all that's left.'

'You go?'

'Better me or Tom than your people or those damned prisoners.'

The shrewd old man repeated something he had said earlier. 'You go, we keep your friend.'

John's patience like the rest of his disposition had been getting more raw as the hours had passed. He looked unwaveringly at the old man. 'You don't trust no one, do you?'

The old man's dark eyes with the muddy whites gave John stare for stare as he said, 'Maybe you don't come back. Maybe they know you are an outlaw. Maybe they hang you. We keep your friend.'

Scar returned and as before ignored John to briefly speak to the spokesman. After he departed this time he told John Indians had caught a man trying to see inside the rock field. He would be along after he had been searched, his weapons taken.

The old man seemed grimly pleased. 'Damn fool white man,' he said, and had no opportunity to elaborate. Scar and the large Indian brought a hatless man forward, knocked him down and stood behind him.

He was young. He was much younger than John and younger than Tom. He was also frightened as he sat on the ground looking longest at John Beeson.

Mexican Horse sent for Bones to interpret which exasperated John. The old devil had been conversing with John in passable English.

When Bones arrived he sat on the ground, ignoring the frightened youth.

The old man used his own language before Bones

faced the frightened youth. 'What is your name?' he asked, and got back a swift, breathless reply, 'Frank Leslie.'

Mexican Horse had Bones interpret again. He wanted to know how many white men were out there and why he had come; he was too young for gun-fighting.

The answer surprised – and pleased – the old Indian. The lad had come with his father, Jeb Smith. His father had told him it was time he learned how to exterminate vermin.

Scar spoke to Mexican Horse. The old man nodded and put his steady stare upon Frank Leslie. He did not use Bones when he addressed the youth. 'How old are you?'

Frank Leslie answered promptly as before. 'Fifteen. Sixteen in four months.'

For the first time the old man turned his attention to John Beeson, who read the old man's expression correctly, and nodded. 'I'll go talk. I'll say the boy dies if I don't return.'

Mexican Horse nodded, then turned his attention back to the youth. John arose and dusted off. He did not like the look on the old man's face, nor the looks of the broncos standing behind Frank Leslie, so he said, 'Don't let nothin' happen to him while I'm gone.'

The old man nodded without taking his narrowed gaze off the youth.

After Beeson's departure Mexican Horse leaned and glared. The youth turned white which was not noticeable in the failing daylight. He said, 'My paw will pay you.' The Indians ignored that. Mexican Horse gestured for the youth to be taken away, then sat a long time in thought before hunting up Tom, who already knew from John what was happening. Mexican Horse said, 'You stay. Don't climb rock no more.'

Scar hunkered fifteen feet away holding his old carbine upright between both knees. Tom leaned against a saddle and said, 'I hope it works.'

Scar sat motionless, impassive and silent.

'Because if it don't, no one'll leave this place tomorrow.'

Still Scar was silent and impassive.

Night settled, there were stars like diamond chips scattered randomly overhead. The moon was coming later this night and would be fuller when it arrived. There was heat but nowhere nearly as much as there had been during the day.

John took no chances. He began calling ahead shortly after leaving the forted-up Indians. When he was about halfway to the brush fire where not a man was visible now, two ghosts appeared silently behind him and remained behind him until he reached the posse-rider camp.

A tall man in a soiled brown duster came from the vicinity of the fire, stopped, stared and said, 'Give me your sidearm.'

John handed it over but the oddly attired man did not move. 'What else you got? Boot-knife, a belly-gun?'

'Never carried either. I come to palaver with your head man.'

The lanky man still did not move. 'You with them In'ians?'

'Yes. Me'n my partner was caught by them.'

'Is that so? An' now you're going to palaver with us for them.'

Furnace Creek

'They're holdin' my partner until I get back.'

'Mister, I don't think you're goin' back.'

A stocky man walked up, ignored the man wearing the duster and asked John's name. He then asked if John rode with the raiding Indians. John shook his head, repeated what he had told the lanky man and was led closer to the dying fire, but not too close, not close enough for any of them to be fire-lighted. Where he stopped there was horse equipment piled in all direction and there was a lot of it. He did not see more than maybe ten or fifteen men, but he could hear others around him in the darkness.

No one had fed the fire recently and greasewood of any kind burns hot and furiously. It was dying when the stocky man gestured for John to sit. The stocky man selected a saddle to sit on. He hadn't sat on the ground in years and had an excellent reason. He asked John his name and got what was probably the predicted rely.

'If it's like you say, them tomahawks caught you, who's the other feller?'

'Tom Jones.'

Men were drifting closer, clearly wary of Indians being in the night somewhere but curious about the white man who had come to their camp. Eventually it became quite a crowd, and John thought someone's estimate of thirty was wrong by close to twice that number.

Even by starlight it was easy to see every man was armed with a belt-gun, some had sheathed knives and all of them had carbines.

He told the stocky man all the Indians wanted was to be free to migrate to Mexico where they intended to stay. The stocky man's expression showed clear hostili-

Furnace Creek

ty when he said, 'It ain't goin' to be that easy, mister. They bushwhacked some fellers an' two of 'em died.' The stocky man had been wearing roping gloves which he now removed slowly and thoughtfully before speaking again. 'I got no idea who you'n your partner are nor what you're doin' with them renegades, but I do know we're not leavin' until those sons of bitches is dead. all of them, bucks, squaws an' pups.'

John waited until silence had settled then said, 'Which one of you gents is named Jeb Smith?'

The stocky man inclined his head without answering. John spoke quietly. 'They got your boy, Mister Smith.'

For a long moment silence lingered then a tall youth said, 'We scouted together, Mister Smith. When I got home I figured he'd already come back.'

The stocky man looked steadily at Beeson. 'What does he look like?'

John described the lad, saw the stocky man's expression change, and said, 'No sense in bringing' a lad that young on somethin' like this.'

The stocky man's reply was almost fierce. 'They got to learn. A boy's no different'n a man in this country. They got to take their chances.'

John slowly looked at the men around them. Several of the older ones were staring hard at the stocky man. John quietly said, 'You crowd them In'ians, mister, an' you'll get your boy back with his head half cut off.' John changed the subject, his trump card hadn't helped, so now he said, 'You got plenty of water have you?'

The stocky man glared in silence.

'They tell me,' John said, 'there's another water-hole

about six, seven miles west of here.'

A bearded man loudly exclaimed, 'Poison water, mister.'

John accepted that and pushed up to his feet addressing the stocky man for the last time. 'You force a fight an' forted-up like they are, with nothin' to lose anyway, they'll fight you to the fare-thee-well, meanwhile your horses'll likely go crazy from thirst. Maybe you'll massacre 'em but you sure-Lord won't do it quick nor easy. They're fightin' little bastards.' John waited for the stocky man to reply but he arose and walked away without a word.

One of those older riders took John aside. 'That ain't his real son. He married the cow an' the calf come with her. She was a crippled lady. A wagon team spooked, she fell astraddle the near side forewheel an' died two weeks later – cryin' her heart out. My missus was with her. She told my missus her man resented the lad, never treated him right an' when she died he'd get even meaner. Now you know why he answered you like he done. I'll tell you why he wouldn't make no trade with you, because he don't give a damn what happens to the boy.'

John eyed the bearded man. 'How about you'n the rest? Even if you whip them In'ians some of you ain't going back. They'll fight to their last breath – for what, mister? They got nothin' you'd want an' all they want is to get over the line into Messico. An' if you whip 'em it won't be easy. Maybe take two or three days. What shape'll your horses be in by then?'

The posse-rider considered John. They were about the same age. He said, 'No one's goin' to like you takin' their side.'

Furnace Creek

'I don't expect they will,' John replied. 'Mister, me'n my partner'll lose no matter who wins. We come with the In'ians as captives. There's five others like us. There was eight but they killed three. You know about bein' between a rock an' a hard place?'

The posse-rider said, 'You couldn't escape?'

John snorted. 'If In'ians ever get hold of you, try it. Just look like you're ponderin' on it, they'll cut your throat before you can swallow.'

The stocky man returned with two other men. He said, 'We're goin' to keep you captive.'

John said, 'If I don't come back they'll kill the lad as sure as we're standin' here.'

The stocky man glared. 'He come along. He took his chances like the rest of us.'

The bearded man turned. 'I'll be damned,' he exclaimed to the stocky man. 'I ain't goin' to stand by an' let you get the lad killed.'

Several other men crowded close to the angry man, expressionless but clearly hostile. For the lad's stepfather the odds piled up. Most of the riders knew the stocky man and knew about his treatment of the boy, but this went beyond a tanning with a quirt.

The stocky man glared at John. 'Go back. Tell our renegade friends the army'll be here tomorrow, day after at the latest. Tell 'em they're bringing' a brass cannon on wheels. They'll blow them rocks to dust. Tell 'em if they come put, put down their guns, we'll turn 'em over to the army, an' most likely they'll be put in a reservation.'

John stared at the stocky man, at some of the others, particularly the bearded man, then turned and started back in the direction of the dimly discernible rocks.

Behind him there was not a sound. Up ahead he knew a dozen sets of black eyes were watching but again, there was not a sound.

Tom was standing with others when John had got back into the rock-bound clearing. Mexican Horse was standing like a shriveled statue looking for all the world like an ancient withered mummy.

John told them what had been said, not word for word but close enough. The big Indian cursed in Spanish. He knew no other way to swear. His native language had no profanity in it.

Mexican Horse stood looking steadily at John, who shrugged and said, 'I done my best.'

That wasn't what the old man was staring about. Children were the only way the band could perpetuate itself. Sons in particular were valued. He did not like white men, had never liked them, but he had no idea until this minute how evil they were. The father would let his son have his throat cut without trying to prevent it.

Mexican Horse walked away. His sister, the woman with the braid, followed him. The other tribesmen scattered, mostly grim and silent. Come daylight they would fight like tigers and if, tomorrow night, they were all dead – they, their women and children, then there was no god, or if there was, he shared with whites antagonism towards Indians.

John and Tom withdrew to a place where no one was too close, sat with their backs to boulders and had a chew. Their plugs were almost down to knuckle size. Bones brought a water gut from which they drank, then Bones sat with them to say, 'They will get my eight horses.' Tom was annoyed but said nothing.

John said, 'Soldiers will get here tomorrow with their cannon. No later than day after tomorrow. Bones, when they unlimber on these rocks maybe you can ride one and lead the others where you an' them horses will be goin'. It don't make no difference to a cannon whether its steel hits horses or men – or women, old folks and kids. Cannon are blind.'

Scar appeared wraith-like, squatted with the gun between his knees and gazed steadily at John, who thought the white-hater wanted to speak but couldn't, so he spoke to him. 'It's no good.'

'They won't trade?'

'No. An' the army's comin' with a cannon.'

'Tomorrow?'

'Or the day after.'

'They will kill you too.'

John nodded, spat aside and returned his gaze to the scar-faced Indian. 'An' the children, the old people, the women.'

Scar sat in long silence before speaking again. 'I tell Mexican Horse we should sneak away while it is dark.'

John shook his head. 'You caught one of 'em. They got this place plumb cut off on all sides.'

'One man could get past,' Scar said, and John agreed. 'Likely he could an' what good would that do? Mexican Horse told me you got no close friendly In'ians.'

Scar was a stubborn individual. 'They got to have water,' he exclaimed.

John answered him curtly. 'They'll get water. They'll lead their horses to the spring over dead In'ians. They'll get water.'

The big Indian came to join them. He too squatted

with a gun between his knees. He said something only Scar and Bones understood and Scar brightened. 'Three In'ians can belly crawl past them, find the horses an' set them loose. Then we can all ride to Messico an' they can't catch us on foot.'

Tom spoke irritably. 'You could be a ghost an' you'd never get near them horses. They'll have a man with every horse or two. Scar, them bastards ain't new to this. They got us in a pocket we can't get out of.'

The big Indian addressed Tom. 'You want to set here an' let 'em kill you? I don't. In the dark all the warriors can run at their camp.'

'An' get yourselves killed for nothin'.'

John looked ahead through the mostly silent camp. some of the older women sat on the ground rocking back and forth. One particular woman caught and held his attention. The sister of Mexican Horse had the captive youth sitting at her side while she fed him slices of jerky.

Somewhere a long way off a wolf howled. There was no answer. An old wizened man smiled in the direction of the sounding wolf and relaxed among his filthy old ragged blankets. He and wolf had met many times. They were kin. He had never killed a wolf and never would. Wolf was man and man was wolf.

Mexican Horse joined them as solemn as an owl. He had painted his forehead black from a soot-sack from his medicine bundle. No one had to explain to the white men the significance of a black forehead.

One of the five captives called for food and water. They were offered water from a gut bag but no food. Hunger could be borne another few hours. After that the captives wouldn't need food.

Furnace Creek

The wolf sounded again, closer this time and the wizened old man broadly smiled to disclose no more than six or seven teeth.

An owl swooped low where he had been in the habit of catching rodents, snakes, birds, anything edible that came for water.

He abruptly beat his wings furiously and disappeared northward beyond the rocks.

7
HEADING FOR DISASTER

It was the waiting. No one slept except that toothless old man. He went to sleep softly smiling. The bucks cleaned their weapons, made sure of ammunition and talked quietly to one another. Every creature on earth has a death song. Mexican Horse and his people were no different, but they would not chant until close to dawn when the inevitable was obvious; until then – who knew – there were spirits. Every person alive had one and all spirits were, like the white man's God, both good and bad. To the people forted up in the puny spring there was no way of knowing which would favour them, so they waited.

Tom went to the bound prisoners to explain the situation. Without dissent each man offered to fight with the Indians. As one said, if the army came the Indians would not stand a chance, but being with them in the rocks meant they would also be killed, and it was better to fight than to sit like sheep waiting to be killed.

Tom sought Mexican Horse and relayed that information. The old man shook his head without speaking. Tom returned to John to curse the old man's stubbornness. John said nothing. He had been watching the woman with braided hair fussing over the fifteen-year-old captive, who seemed both afraid and comfortable. It was doubtful if he had ever seen real Indians before, the wild ones called renegades. Nor could he have felt reassured by visible preparations for war.

He was a good-looking youth who now would never have to shave. John's resentment against the boy's stepfather grew by the hour.

When Tom came up and sat down the older man said, 'I forgot somethin'. The plunder. There's enough in them Mex packs to make them possemen live easy for a long time, providin' they could sell that –'

Tom interrupted. 'They couldn't be bought if what they said to you was serious talk. They lost three men an' got humiliated by that ambush.'

John agreed but for a different reason. The lad's stepfather was one of those unyielding sons of bitches who wouldn't be bought or browbeaten no matter how pointless his course was and regardless of how many suffered and died, even his own acquaintances.

A very old Indian with a few discoloured snags for teeth came over where they sat, dragging a filthy old ragged blanket. Without a word, he sat, wrapped the blanket around himself and smiled at Beeson and Ellison. He said something in his own language but without Bones to interpret John and Tom sat gazing stoically at the old man. Eventually he began to gently rock and chant. It bothered Tom so he arose and went toward the water-hole where some stronghearts were holding a council. Every one of them had a black forehead and shiny clean weapons. Mexican Horse was talking when Tom arrived and squatted. The Indians ignored him.

Bones was with the five bound prisoners who regarded him from expressionless faces. Eventually one man said, 'Is the old man goin' to give us guns an' turn us loose?'

Bones did not think so but he was tactful when he replied, 'It won't matter. Five guns won't make no difference. The army's comin' with cannon.'

Another prisoner swore fiercely before glaring at Bones as he said, 'You damned raghead In'ians! We're right good marksmen. Me'n Jake, the feller beside me, was in the war. We was sharpshooters. We can take out them cannoneers every time one steps up to load'n fire. You tell that shrivelled old bastard what I said. An' somethin' else, we been around In'ians a long time an' yet to see one that can shoot worth a damn. Make heaps of noise an' get excited, but never hit nothin' unless by accident. Go tell the old man what I said.'

Bones lingered, sat gazing at the filthy, unshaven, villainous looking captives, smiled and eventually walked away – not in the direction of the council where Tom squatted with the warriors and Mexican Horse, but rather where John Beeson sat slightly apart.

He told John what the captive had said and John spoke without looking over where the captives sat. 'Turn them men loose an' we'll have folks inside the rocks gettin' shot as well as them outside shooting in.'

'You know them?' Bones asked and got a sour reply.

'I know their kind. They're hired manhunters. some years back their kind collected scalps for bounty. You arm them inside the rocks an' when the fightin' starts they'll kill In'ians, an' if they survive, the army an' them other bastards will make heroes out of 'em.'

Furnace Creek

Something in the faintly brush-fired camp of posse-riders caught the attention of the Indians; shod-horses in motion. Mexican Horse's council broke up. John arose to cock his head and listen but now the Indians were making too much noise so he went over to the rock where a scout was lying, climbed up and cocked his head. The Indian nearby turned and said, 'Many riders.'

John ignored that. What held his full attention was not the riders but the direction they were riding – northward. Tom got up there beside him with Scar. For as long as they could hear the horsemen not a word was said, but when the sounds grew faint, Tom spoke. 'Goin' to find the soldiers an' lead 'em down here.'

John did not answer.

Scar hunkered with the old gun between his knees. He and the scout exchanged a few guttural words. Bones and Mexican Horse climbed the rock, which left very little room. They were also silent. The riders did not slacken their gait even when it became difficult to hear them.

Someone threw dry manzanita into the fire of the posse-riders. Flames flared instantly. By their light the watchers on the rock saw men moving.

Tom made another guess – wrong this time too. He said, 'It's got to be the army's comin'. They're fixin' to attack us as soon as the soldiers get here.'

John squatted, unmindful of his left knee which hurt every time he did this. Mexican Horse squatted at his side and raised an arm. 'Not many at fire.'

Tom took this up. 'Now'd be a good time to hit 'em. Before the others get back with the soldiers.'

What John had trouble with was so many men going

Furnace Creek

to find the army, even in darkness it would not require more than three or four riders to locate the soldiers. What he and the others had heard was a lot more than three or four men. It had sounded to John more like about half the posse-riders.

An idea formed. More hopeful than logical. He told Mexican Horse to keep the fighting men ready, that he was going to scout the posse-rider camp.

The old man nodded, did not even turn to watch John climb down and move out of the rocks where darkness hid him well except when he was moving. There was enough starlight and moon-glow to show movement, but he had no trouble. He even got among the hobbled horses which were close to the camp. From there he estimated that close to half the animals were gone, and the men around the fire seemed also to be fewer in number.

If there were guards out John did not find them and he looked because if there were, and they got between John and the rocks he would have trouble.

He went westerly a fair distance then circled around northward. He was careful, stopping often to listen. He saw no guards and heard nothing, except once when he was making a wide sashay far from the fire on his way back to the rocks.

A wolf howled.

The Indians, with Tom, were waiting. John told them he had no idea why, but about half the posse riders had been in that party of horsemen they had heard riding north.

Tom said, 'We can get 'em. Half ain't much more'n us. In the dark we can get up there an' clean their damned ploughs.'

Bones interpreted and several warriors growled approval of the idea, but neither John nor Mexican Horse did. In fact the old man acted as though Tom had not spoken. He gave several curt and guttural orders. For moments afterward the fighting Indians stood staring at the old man but Mexican Horse did not relent. The next time he spoke he used Spanish. '*Vaminos, pronto!*'

The Indians moved clear heading for their ragged camps. Tom looked after the old man, finally faced John and said, 'Are we goin' after 'em? What did the old screwt say?'

Bones answered. 'He say strike camp. Hurry. We go to Messico.'

The camp became a scene of chaos again, but this time there was recognizable order. It required nearly an hour before the old man astride a tucked-up bay horse led the exodus out of the forted-up place. Not a sound was made. Even the half-wild dogs slunk along silently. After an hour of steady riding Mexican Horse dropped back beside John and spoke in English, fractured but understandable. 'We go. Scar far back. We get there.' He leaned and shoved out a skinny arm, grasped John's arm half way to the elbow then rode up ahead and they did not meet again until a stumpy bronco came back from the south and told the old man he thought he had heard a white-man bugle.

After that the band veered westerly and held to that course until the faint chill which presaged dawn was noticeable. They were still east of the Furnace Creek country and the desert, and there was horse feed, tall, almost knee-high to a mounted man, some kind of pale grass which had seeded heads on incredibly long, fragile stalks.

John watched horses and mules trying to snatch mouthfuls on the way and rode up to Mexican Horse to say if Scar hadn't reported pursuit from the north, they had better rest and let the animals eat. The old man looked back, then easterly, the direction the scout had thought he had heard a bugle. John reined to a halt, swung off and let his horse greedily browse on a loose rein.

The old man looked down. John looked back. The old man knew men, regardless of colour they were the same in many ways. The outlaw he called Juan was not going to continue riding until the animal he was riding had eaten.

The old man raised a scrawny arm, slid sideways from his mount and followed John Beeson's example; he walked slowly along allowing his starved mount to clip grass heads. The others did the same, without a lot of noise and with wary glances over their shoulders. But even when they put ears to the ground there were no reverberations. If the posse-riders were coming after them they were too far back to reach the band before they got over the line into Mexico.

But there was impatience. Any people to whom existence was harsh and hand-to-mouth had no compassion for dumb animals, unless as in this situation they had to favour the livestock or very probably lose out altogether.

The prisoners had trudged afoot. They were staggering and glassy-eyed by the time the others walked with their animals who browsed as they went. One of the captives suddenly pitched forward and made no attempt to rise.

Furnace Creek

The Indians trudged past indifferently. This was something else they knew about first-hand. Death came when it wished to. It always had and always would. Whatever the reason, the dead were gone, everyone else had to keep moving.

Another bound captive called to John Beeson, who went back. The captive was that greying man with a full beard. His eyes were sunken, his lips chapped and bleeding. If he was the strongest of the captives more would drop dead from neglect and exhaustion.

John gave the bearded man water. He also gave him a corner of his diminishing tobacco plug. The greying man sounded like a frog when he said, 'Shoot us an' get this over with.'

John offered more water which the captive drank around his cud of Mule Shoe. Afterwards, feeling better if not necessarily stronger he spoke again. 'It's on'y goin' to end one way for me'n the others. If them posse-men don't catch up the army might, an' if it don't, mister, the Messicans'll kill a man for his boots. Get this over with right here. There ain't no more future for you'n your partner than there is for us. Any way you look at it we're dead meat, an' we can't keep goin'. We're wore out.'

John fed water to the other captives, heard what they had to say which was pretty much as the bearded man had said. He went back to lead his animal along and Bones came up also leading a horse. He was glum. 'My eight horses . . . .'

'What about 'em?'

'They're goin' to die from hunger pretty soon. If the cowmen or the army don't kill them an' all of us first.'

Scar appeared from the north, saw what others were

Furnace Creek

doing and swung off to allow his horse to crop feed on a loose rein. He led the horse up where Mexican Horse was squatting in thought while his horse grazed loose dragging the reins.

They talked while Scar let his horse also wander on a loose rein. It was a long palaver before Scar arose, caught his animal and led it away grazing as it went.

Scar passed Tom and John. He did an uncustomary thing, he threw them a wave. They waved back. John said, 'Like it or not, we're part of the band.'

Tom offered no reply.

Eventually Mexican Horse got back astride, the others also. Mexican Horse did not push ahead, he rode with slack reins allowing his mount to snatch browse as it went along.

The chill increased and off in the sooty east John thought he caught sight of a faint bank of pewter-coloured light all along the far curve of the earth. He sought Bones to ask how much farther to the border. Bones's reply was encouraging. 'Maybe a mile, maybe not.' Mexican Horse's sister passed with the captured lad at her side. She was trading words with him. She would point to a mule, say its name in her language, then the lad would say the name in English which the woman would repeat struggling with enunciation.

She did not really care to learn English, and in fact she already knew some words in English.

John watched them and wondered if the woman wasn't working at keeping the boy's mind off his predicament – or – whether she had found someone close enough to the age of her dead son to help mitigate the anguish of loss.

His surmises were correct, both of them.

Furnace Creek

The chill drove no one in search of more clothing. It never got that cold in the Furnace Creek country, or westward some miles where the desert ran southward to the border and down over it for many miles.

They all watched the slow, inexorable spread of that pewter light. They fearfully kept a rearward vigil. Eventually two bucks and Scar returned to report there was no party of pursuing riders or, if there was, they were too far back to reach the Indians before they got down into Mexico.

Mexican Horse extended the period of time for the horses to be browsed along. No one protested and only rarely did an Indian look up their back trail which, with new-day light would show unmistakable tracks from the rocked-up place toward Mexico.

Tom slouched along chewing jerky. He did not look much like the man John Beeson had partnered-up with some years earlier. His cheeks were beard-stubbled, his eyes were sunken, his cheeks seemed hollow in that puny, corpse-coloured dawn.

John said, 'Somewhere we got to leave 'em.'

Tom replied without looking at John. 'Yeah, an' by now they got lawmen'n bounty hunters an' maybe even soldiers lookin' for two renegade whites travellin' with raiders. We was in trouble before, when we first got down here, but partner, we're in one hell of a lot more trouble now. From what I've heard the gov'ment an' the army don't take kindly to whites riding with In'ians.'

John waited until it had all been said then spoke. 'We got to split off soon. Go west, hole-up for a spell then figure where we're goin' next.'

Tom faced the older man. 'What about Texas?'

Furnace Creek

'I got a bad feelin' about ridin' the border-country all the way to Texas.'

'Go west, then?'

'We can't go north. I'd say go west, angle away from the border country and stay clear of settlements.'

The Indians were moving wearily and stoically, especially the old ones. The animals perked up a little but not much. Enough, John thought to get them down into Mexico. He began watching the westerly country as dawn-light brightened. What he saw was not encouraging. The desert of the Furnace Creek country ran directly down into Mexico.

Tom wagged his head about this. 'I tell you, John, since that last hold-up we been steadily gettin' closer'n closer to a bad end, and that damned desert will set us afoot as sure as I'm a foot tall. These horses is coastin' on grit an' grass-heads. The grit might get 'em a little farther but what they ate back yonder'll be used up before noon – and that's when we'll be crossin' that damned desert.'

This time everyone heard the bugle. Its sound came from the east, and south.

The Indians did not stop their nightmare exodus but they looked toward the steadily increasing light. They saw nothing, light was not clear enough yet for good visibility, but sound could travel in a silent world for many miles.

Mexican Horse stopped angling and turned directly south. He and several other Indians held a guttural discussion after which several Indians rode away to scout.

To John and Tom, and those bedraggled four bound captives the bugle meant different things. To them the sound of a bugle brought them straight up looking eastward, to Tom and his partner it meant one more danger and as Tom had mentioned earlier, unless they reached the line soon and got over it into Mexico, the best they could expect from soldiers was to be blindfolded and shot as renegade whites riding with renegade Indians.

The scouts who left riding eastward returned too soon. John swore and stood in his stirrups. He could distantly make out pale dust but visibility was not good enough yet for him to be convinced he was not imagining that. He sat down in the saddle and watched the Indians. They dredged up new strength from somewhere, even the old people took longer strides and those who were mounted pushed their horses into a shambling trot.

Mexican Horse dropped back to ride with John and Tom. He had Scar and a clearly distraught Bones with him. He spoke so fast Bones had trouble interpreting. 'He say soldiers tryin' to get a line strung across the border in front of us.'

John accepted that. Bones and his kind used smoke signals, which worked very well but nowhere nearly as well as telegraph lines.

He asked how much father and the old man raised his scrawny arm pointing southward. 'Half mile.'

Scar spoke in English 'We can run for it.'

Even Mexican Horse looked at Scar with scorn. John put it into words. 'Not on these animals.'

8
THE LONGEST NIGHT

John heard shod horses moving southward. He squinted but could not yet see much. Tom also heard and said, 'Son of a bitch. They got us cut off.'

Mexican Horse had to also have heard those southerly sounds but he kept on riding. Bones was beside him. The old man said something and kept on riding. Bones dropped back to John and Tom to say, 'Mexican Horse singing death chant.'

John rode ahead, got beside the old man and said, 'Talk. All we got left is to palaver.'

The old man turned sunken, tired eyes on John and replied in English. 'Too late. Army don't talk. Army shoot,' and faced forward to continue his chant.

Tom and Bones came forward. Not far behind Scar rode dutifully, still the guard, even though shortly now there would be no need.

Tom spoke to his partner. 'We should've left 'em a mile back.'

John jerked his thumb rearward without speaking. Scar was back there.

Up ahead it was beginning to brighten up enough for

movement to show. Every eye was on the blue wraiths riding from east to west.

Easier to see because they were whitewashed was a boundary marker of piled stones. Up ahead a soldier with a companion who carried a little guidon banner turned northward at a walk. They became clearly visible to the tribesmen as Mexican Horse held up an arm to bring his people to a halt.

Where the officer and his enlisted companion drew rein was directly in front of Mexican Horse, a distance of about fifty or sixty feet. The officer was young, his enlisted companion was older, bronzed and seasoned.

Mexican Horse called John forward. Light was increasing by the minute. At sight of the white man both soldiers stiffened. Bones trailed after John and Mexican Horse spoke directly to him. Bones hesitated about interpreting because the soldiers would understand when he used English. He said something back to Mexican Horse and got a dark look and guttural growl from the old man.

Bones then interpreted in English. 'He says he will not surrender.'

The soldiers sat like carvings. They had big American horses as slick as moles. In fact in every way the contrast between them and the tribesmen was clear even in poor light.

The officer leaned forward in his McClellen saddle to address Mexican Horse, which the old man responded to by silence and a steady black-eyed stare. Bones sighed. This was one of those times when the spokesman would not use English, so Bones interpreted aware that the spokesman already knew what the soldier had said.

Furnace Creek

He spoke to the old man quietly. 'Soldiers say you put down all guns – and knives.'

Mexican Horse glared making no move to drop either his carbine or his knife.

Bones acted like a man with a hot potato in his britches.

When the officer repeated his demand that the Indians disarm themselves Bones interpreted the order with white knuckles holding his reins.

Mexican Horse glanced sideways to see who had come up on his right side. It was John Beeson looking as sober as a judge.

Both soldiers stared at John a long moment before the officer repeated his order for the Indians to put down their weapons.

As before the old man acted deaf and defiant. The officer did not make the demand again. Actually, he was killing time. The soldiers from the east had not yet sealed off the border. He wanted to palaver until that had been accomplished. He nodded in John's direction. 'Your name, mister?'

'John Smith. My partner back yonder is Tom Jones.'

The officer's eyes perceptibly narrowed. 'Likely names,' the officer said and spoke before John could reply. 'You'll be the white men riding with these raiders.'

'My partner'n me was caught by the Indians. The only ridin' we done with 'em was to trail this far south. If you're goin' to make us out renegades, ask the In'ians how we come to be with 'em.'

The officer had decent light to see by. He considered the Indians, the starving animals, saw a white youth and asked John who he was and how he'd come to be

Furnace Creek

with the Indians.

John explained cryptically. When he had finished the officer looked back, looked at his guidon-bearer, then returned his attention to John.

'I was told you'n your partners are outlaws an' for me to fetch you back.'

Mexican Horse was getting impatient. He could see those whitewashed piles of rock. They were no more than a few hundred feet distant. He said something sharp to Bones, whose knuckles turned even whiter. He stared at the old man, craned around where Indians were beginning to sift away, bucks in one place, women and pups in another. Mexican Horse had said for the warriors to prepare to fight.

The guidon-bearer, an old campaigner, spoke low to the officer, whose reply was to swear at the other soldier and exclaim that bunch of ragged, starved-out, black-eyed, unwashed bronco renegades would obey his orders or take the consequences.

John spoke to the officer. 'Mister, these ain't town In'ians. They've been fightin' all their lives. Push 'em an' you'll be the first sittin' duck to get killed.'

The older soldier spoke again to the officer, this time more loudly. 'Leave it be, Lieutenant. They ain't goin' nowhere.'

The officer reddened. He glared in long silence. Scar and the big Indian knelt, aimed squarely at his chest and cocked their ancient carbines.

The guidon-bearer became rigid in his saddle. 'Lieutenant!'

Through the silence could be heard more shod horses arriving. It was light enough for the Indians to watch them ride down a long line and take their places.

Furnace Creek

Back among the Indians Tom said, 'Gawda' mighty!'

Mexican Horse began chanting again, but it sounded more like a moan and it was not loud. The old man had his carbine firmly across his lap in the saddle.

The officer spun his horse and rode southward as though he had a ramrod up his back.

John sighed, the bucks with aimed carbines eased hammers down and watched the departing soldiers. Mexican Horse looked at John as he said, 'No good.'

John nodded and replied quietly, 'You done your best. A man can't do more.'

Scar came up on foot, the old man leaned and the stocky Indian said something in his ear, then walked away leaving Mexican Horse to straighten atop the horse and looked bitterly at the blue line which was now clearly visible in detail.

He slid off his horse, turned his back on John and went among his tribesmen.

John also dismounted but he led his animal where Tom was. His partner'd had an idea earlier and mentioned it now. 'Why didn't the old gaffer trade them four posse-riders for us to get down over the line?'

John had no idea why the old man hadn't made that offer, but his hunch was that Mexican Horse thought this new day was to be his last, and was ready for it to be that way. Nothing else mattered any more.

The people removed packs, made a loose camp and those who were hungry ate, the others sat like condemned people looking blank.

Scar approached John and Tom, squatted and said, 'We can sneak past 'em after dark.'

Tom looked doubtful. From where he was sitting he could see more soldiers than he'd seen in many years.

99

Furnace Creek

John gave a delayed retort to the scarred Indian. 'You can try,' he said.

Scar bristled. 'We steal horses tied next to riders.'

John did not doubt that nor was he convinced that no matter how alert and numerous the soldiers would be after dark the Indians could not sneak past them. The distance was no more than a couple of hundred yards.

Tom, though, squinting at the blue cordon was of the opinion even a snake could not get past them and said so. Scar gave Ellison a pitying look and departed. They watched him going among the other fighting men. Tom shook his head but before he could speak John said, 'It's their choice, an' I'll give you odds most of 'em won't live to reach no reservation, an' they know it.'

'What about the ones left behind? I still think old Bones should have traded the possemen for free passage.'

'Tom, that officer wouldn't give his mother a drink of water if she was dyin' of thirst.'

The young lad came over, shyly stood until Tom gestured for him to sit, which he then did and asked a question. 'Where are the fellers my step-paw brought down here?'

No one had an answer and John, for one, thought that was the least of the present concerns. He asked the lad if he liked the woman with the braided hair, and the boy nodded. 'Can't understand her hardly, but she's like a mother.'

The sun was climbing when the camp had an unexpected visitor. The old campaigner who had accompanied the officer as guidon-bearer walked into the camp. They had to assume he was armed but his belt-holster

Furnace Creek

was one of those with a flap.

Some Indians stared, some glared and the rest did what Indians do best, they totally ignored the soldier. To those people he did not appear to exist.

Mexican Horse sat and waited but the soldier, who wore a sergeant's chevrons went instead where Tom and John were sitting. He sat down, nodded and said, 'You fellers the only whites they got?'

Tom answered quickly. 'No. There's the lad yonder with that woman, an' four possemen.' Tom leaned for emphasis when he continued. 'Mister, these In'ians kill their prisoners an' the boy as well.'

'An' maybe you gents too?'

Tom shrugged. 'John'n me been gettin' closer to the Pearly Gates ever since we come into this country and that's a fact. Right now we got the army in front, most likely posse-riders behind us, an' far as I know more soldiers easterly.'

The sergeant fished inside his tunic, brought forth two Mexican cigars, handed one to Tom first then to John, dug out one for himself and held the lucifer for all the stogies to be lighted. When he had a good head of smoke rising the soldier removed his cigar and said, 'I'm goin' on retirement next spring an' of all the God forsaken places to get killed this is the worst I've ever seen.'

John waited for more, but the soldier sat and smoked so John asked a question. 'Does that officer know you come here?'

'No. Only a couple of other old-timers who'll be retirin' soon know. Why?'

'Because what I saw of him, if he knew you was settin' here with us he'd have you skinned alive.'

101

Furnace Creek

The sergeant's teeth flashed in a broad smile. 'There's more the lieutenant don't know than could be filled in ten big books. He's a West Pointer. Me, I been over twenty years at it, through the war, scuffled with my share of tomahawks an' Messicans an' this close to retirin' damned if I could see the sense of him forcin' your broncos to fight. They wouldn't win, you boys know that, but you two might get hurt an' I might. I only got to stay clear of trouble until spring.'

John said, 'How do we stop a fight?'

The sergeant tipped ash, considered the glowing end of his cigar, then looked straight at John and said, 'Forget the border an' Messico. Even if you charged for it you'd lose maybe half your people an' the survivors would get massacred by *rurales* over the line.'

The soldier leaned forward and also said, 'Sneak back the way you come. Do it tonight. You can make it far enough to buy yourself a full day before we come huntin' you.'

John said, 'Not on our horses, mister. They're starvin'. They could maybe get over the line but just barely an' afterwards they'd start droppin' like flies.'

The sergeant considered the glowing tip of his cigar. He seemed to be having trouble between what he wanted to say and what he could be shot for saying. In the balance was retirement in a few months. He blew out a rough breath, raised his eyes to John and spoke quietly.

'Our line runs east'n west about a mile. The figurin' is that you don't have enough In'ians to go that far in either direction. The figurin' is that you'll make a direct charge through us in the centre. That's where the lieutenant's built up the reserve.'

The sergeant let the cigar go out. He was clearly

Furnace Creek

having trouble. In twenty years he had never once even thought of betrayal so it came hard now, but when he resumed talking he committed himself to a firing squad if he were found out, so the words were crisp.

'In'ians is clever bastards. I've fought 'em from Montana to this God-forsaken country. Your bucks can sneak around our line in the dark. They're damned good at things like that. Sneak around, get below the border then come back an' run off our horses. You understand?'

John nodded.

The sergeant had more to propose but could not bring himself to do it. He dropped the dead cigar, nodded and walked away in the darkness leaving John and Tom silently thoughtful, until John arose, dusted his britches and said, 'Twenty years. A man's luck runs out some time, an' he's right. This is a hell of a country to die in over raggedy-assed In'ians in a fight that won't settle nothin'. What he said is exactly what Scar wants to do.'

He walked over where Mexican Horse and several of his fighting men were sitting in glum silence. Only two of them acknowledged his presence when he sat among them. They were Scar and Mexican Horse.

He spoke quietly without haste and gradually the Indians looked steadily at him. When he had finished one bronco asked a question of the spokesman. The old man nodded and used English to John.

'How do you know this?'

Scar spoke before John could. 'Soldier that come to camp. Him and this one talked a long time.'

Mexican Horse looked at John without speaking until John nodded, then the old man leaned to draw

Furnace Creek

marks in the dust. As he did this Bones and the big buck arrived, listened to what they were told and the large Indian looked over the spokesman's shoulder until the lines on the ground were finished then he said he would take ten men and go east.

Scar volunteered to do the same in the west. This had all been said in their own language but John made a good guess about what they were saying, which was supported by what the old man also told them in their own language. The big Indian and Scar left the council without another word and Mexican Horse raised his black eyes with their muddy whites to John. In English he said, 'It be done.'

John nodded back and arose to depart. He also used English when he said, 'Good. But the darkness will not last forever', and returned where Tom was chewing jerky. As he sat down Tom held out a piece of pepper-cured meat. John took it and chewed in silence. Eventually he said, 'If they get caught we're goners.'

Tom's reply was basically true. 'We're goners anyway no matter what they do.'

There was a slight period of movement among the Indians until the stalkers had been selected and briefed. After they disappeared in the night things returned to dismal normalcy, the only difference, and it was slight, was that all talk seemed to diminish.

That old gummer with the frayed blanket passed where Tom and John were sitting, paused and said, 'Wolf say we make it.'

Tom watched the old man and his dragging blanket walk toward a group of Indians and wagged his head. 'Crazy as a damned coot.'

John was too occupied with his jerky to comment.

Furnace Creek

The longer a person chewed jerky, even a small piece of it, the larger it became. Perhaps that was why it was filling.

Bones came up, squatted and said, 'Why did that soldier do that?'

John smiled tiredly without answering. He doubted that Bones would understand and in any case it would not matter, unless something happened and the army discovered what the sergeant had done, something John preferred not to dwell on. He told Bones if Scar and the other hold-outs got over the line and could sneak back among the horses, it would be a damned miracle.

Bones shook his head. 'They been sneakin' up on deer, buffler an' antelope all their lives. Soldiers . . . .' Bones made a gesture of contempt.

After Bones departed and they had finished the jerky Tom went in search of a water-gut. That was the other effect of jerky, it caused immediate thirst. While he was gone Mexican Horse's sister came to sit with John. She had the boy with her. Communication would be difficult, but the lad, like most children his age, learned quickly and easily. He could not interpret well but well enough. When the woman spoke the boy said, 'She's teachin' me their death song.' The boy seemed uncomfortable. 'She said tomorrow we all die. Me an' you, her an' me.'

John's reply was less hopeful than philosophical. 'We all die, but she may be wrong, boy. If she ain't, well, if you live to my age you'll sometimes wonder if dyin' might not be better'n livin'. Look around you. This ain't livin', this is makin' it a day at a time, havin' nothin', an' bein' scairt all the time.' He stopped talking and smiled at the lad. 'You tell her none of us is dead until we can't talk no more.'

The lad had difficulty interpreting it all but the woman with the big braid in back picked up the gist and looked quizzically at the white man, She said something brusque and this time the boy hung fire. He had understood her and he was supposed to repeat her words to the older man. Respect for elders was ingrained in his generation.

John asked if he had understood and the lad nodded without looking up. 'She asked – are you married? Do you have a woman?'

John laughed, something which brought many dark eyes in his direction. This of all nights was not a time for laughter.

John ignored the staring people and said, 'No, an' I don't aim to be – never.'

This time when the lad interpreted the woman sat for a moment, then sprang to her feet, herded the lad in front and marched briskly away.

Time passed. There was sound down along the boundary line. That many horse soldiers could not have avoided making noise, but it was subdued sound, sentries trading challenges, horses squealing, moving under guard, someone among the soldiers playing a mouth harp.

It was probably one of the older campaigners because the song was one sung by both sides during the Civil War. Its name was *Lorena*.

9
GUNFIRE !

For John and Tom waiting was something they were accustomed to. For the other white captives whose neglect and suffering was very real, it was not. One of them began singing. It was a harmless thing to do but two Indians silenced him by standing with drawn knives.

The greying, bearded man told him to be quiet. He obeyed but in the next moment asked the Indians for food and water. Mexican Horse was passing, understood and gave two orders; the posse-riders were to be fed, and their arms were to be cut loose.

The orders were obeyed but not happily and as the men ate jerky and drank water, those two bucks squatted in front of them with their knives in hand.

The bearded man called, 'Hey, John.'

Beeson arrived and sat on the ground. The captive posse-riders looked terrible even by the poor light. He offered the bearded man his plug. The man eyed the plug which was small, and nibbled off only one ragged corner, returned the plug and said, 'You know what the army'll do to you sidin' with these renegades?'

Furnace Creek

John nodded without speaking. The man who had been singing spoke to the bearded man. 'We ain't in no better way.'

The bearded man ignored that statement. He considered Beeson thoughtfully before saying, 'We maybe got a chance but you got none. If the army or the ragheads don't kill you, there's a lot of cowmen who will.'

Again John nodded but he spoke this time. 'Mister, when we're all so close to dyin' no matter what the odds they ain't no better for you than for Tom an' me.'

One of the other bound men agreed in a coarse voice. 'An' I could've been a farrier up north in a nice little town.'

One of the other four, a thin, fine-boned man with receding hair spoke almost as though what impended had already happened. What John did not know and would never know, was this bounty-rider had been a priest. He was also an alcoholic, and because those two factors were not compatible he had been defrocked. The rest of it, his last seven years, had been a nightmare of inner torture.

He looked straight ahead when he said, 'Mister, do you believe in God?'

John's eyes widened on this captive. He did not have an immediate reply. The bearded man made a humourless smile at John. 'Him'n me argued about that many times. How about you; you a believer?'

John's shock had passed. 'Nothin' to argue about,' he told them. 'Come daylight an' we'll most likely know whether there is one or there ain't one.'

He returned to the place he and Tom had staked out, got comfortable and watched the camp. A few Indians, mostly old ones, were curled into blankets but the

Furnace Creek

majority either sat like stones or softly chanted.

There were stars overhead in a flawless vault of darkness. The moon might come later. That old man who dragged a dirty old blanket was sitting where John could see his face, and he was smiling like someone who knew a profound secret, or maybe who was one brick shy of a load.

Mexican Horse came up, squatted until Bones arrived at his side then spoke gutturally. Bones interpreted. 'He say you make good In'ians. He sorry you go with the rest of us when the army attacks.'

John had had enough of this morbid talk and changed the subject. He asked if the spokesman had heard from Scar. Mexican Horse did not await the interpretation. He shook his head and said, 'Maybe soon now.'

John doubted that. What the scouts were doing would take a lot of time. It wasn't like walking upright in darkness, and the distance was considerable just to get beyond the soldier lines and afterwards to creep far enough beyond it to come back and find the horses. In fact, while John recognized the mastery of stealth of Indians, he was also of the opinion that the army's old campaigners understood this too.

He asked about the bound men. Mexican Horse bypassed Bones again and answered in English. 'Leave 'em.' The old man then said, 'You go. Take saddle-bags an' go.'

Tom sat straighter but John gazed at the spokesman when he said, 'You got no horses that'd carry us five miles.'

The old man was obdurate. This time when he said the same thing he slashed the air with one arm. 'Now.

Go. Horses take you far enough.' He arose. 'Now you go!' he said and was turning away when the woman with the braid came over with the boy. She ignored her brother, pushed the lad toward John and Tom and left him there. When he would have followed her the old man caught him by the shoulder, turned the boy and glared. 'You go with Juan and his amigo. You understand? You go with them now!'

The spokesman went among the Indians, gave an order to a man sitting hunched inside a blanket and walked away. The bronco arose. He moved like someone in a trance.

Bones remained with John and Tom looking worried. 'Too much time gone by,' he murmured and went where several Indians were sitting to drop down among them.

John said he didn't think the scouts could get near the horses for the very least another hour. Tom nodded without speaking.

Excepting normal sounds made by people and horses the night was still as death.

No fires were built, no Indian fires, no soldier fires.

It was a time of waiting and speculation, a time for reflection and making peace with oneself.

Bones returned to say Mexican Horse was angry that the white men were still sitting there. He also said he would pick out the best two horses and bring them back.

John jutted his jaw in the direction of the boy and said, 'Three horses.'

Bones departed, convinced finally he would never have his eight horses, one of the most crushing disappointments of his life. An Indian brought the saddle-bags closer. They were heavy. He sat back and when

Furnace Creek

Bones appeared leading three horses, they made squaw bridles of rope and got astride. The lad mounted bareback with the least difficulty. A number of Indians came up to watch impassively, clutching their blankets close.

Mexican Horse arrived, hoisted the saddle-bags behind John and stepped back. He said something and was raising an arm to start the astride men on their way, when all hell broke loose in the direction of the border.

Guns fired in what seemed to be random, blind shooting. Men yelled. Distinctly audible through all the turmoil was the sound of running horses.

The Indians, Tom and John were like stone carvings, motionless and silent.

The gunfire continued. It seemed to come from many directions. One bull-bassed man who sounded like a trumpet swore and yelled that the raiders had run east. This sounded as though it prompted a general eastward rush.

The Indians slowly twisted, following the sound of men running. One of them said something. No one took it up, they were following the sound of running men very carefully, right up until an Indian spoke, then the crowd loosened a little. What he had told the others was that Scar and the others would not run east, they would run straight north where their tribesmen were. Whether this was true or not the Indians appeared to accept it.

Gunfire continued. It sounded as though individuals were firing at random, unlike the concerted fire which had erupted at the beginning of the turmoil.

Mexican Horse yelled at the Indians who were standing motionless wherever they had been when the firing began. He yelled fiercely for them to leave everything but their weapons and run for the border.

John watched this sudden frenzy of activity. The boy said, 'Concha,' and pointed. The sister of Mexican Horse had a small bundle slung over her back by a thong. She had an unwieldy old Sharps rifle – not a carbine – in one hand and an equally as outdated big hawgleg pistol in her other hand. She went with the others like a flight of ungainly birds directly toward the border, and the thin line of soldiers more concerned with following the easterly sound of a running gunfight did not see the horde of ragged wraiths until the Indians were almost among them. Mexican Horse fired first, then used his old single-shot Sharps as a club.

John, Tom and the boy were rooted. In the darkness muzzleblasts showed, otherwise there were only faint sightings amid yells.

Bones was one of the last to make the charge. He was trying to drive horses ahead. Some older people had not joined the rush, they remained sitting in their blankets following the turmoil by sound, unwilling to leave camp.

Tom leaned, tapped John's arm and jerked his head. They rode westerly on an angling northerly course. It was as dark as the inside of a boot.

They passed through good grass and browse country which was east of the desolate Furnace Creek country.

The boy rode with them. Only he twisted in the saddle occasionally to listen to the gunfire. John and Tom heard it but concentrated on riding.

When they were finally able to do so, they halted to let the animals graze. Tom wanted to push ahead but John simply shook his head. If they were going to

Furnace Creek

escape they had to favour the animals.

About an hour later they heard horses coming behind them. John looked frantically for shelter but visibility was too short to see anything more than a hundred or so feet ahead. He gauged the course of the horses and veered more northward.

With no idea of what they might find they came across a cluster of oaks at the base of a knoll and stopped for the sake of their animals, dismounted and listened. The horses continued due west until it seemed that they were scattering, even stopping in places.

Tom made a good guess 'Loose stock.'

Tom and the boy would have remounted but John held a hand aloft while standing beside his Indian horse. He said, 'Boy, mind the animals. Tom, bring ropes an' come with me.'

The moon had arisen sometime previously but did not increase visibility very much. The men could no longer hear gunfire and for the time being spent no time speculating on whether the Indians had got across the line into Mexico.

They had, but not all of them. Mexican Horse survived but his sister, Scar and others did not. Bones might have if he hadn't tried to keep his little band of horses together, and in order to do this had sashayed back and forth instead of riding hard southward.

He was shot off his horse by a youthful soldier younger than Bones had been. His horses fled westward where the scent of graze was strong. Tom saw the horses first, stopped and brushed his partner's arm. They put ropes around their necks after the custom of men wanting to catch loose horses; a coiled rope in the hand would spook loose stock every time.

Several horses either saw or scented them – most likely the latter – and began sidling clear. One particular animal, large and in good flesh but a little tucked up, raised its head with grass protruding from both sides of its mouth, and watched the two-legged things. It began chewing the grass and dropped its head to crop more, paid no more attention to the men, and Tom got his shank around its neck while the animal was grazing.

John tried to chum his way up to a rawboned big sorrel but that animal was one that could not be caught outside of a corral and sidled away each time John approached. He passed several other animals, finally gave up on the sorrel and captured one of the animals he had passed by.

The third horse was caught easily but would not lead until Tom got behind with a stick, and even then it kept the shank tight all the way back to where the lad was waiting.

They turned their starved Indian horses loose, rigged the captured animals and continued on a northwesterly ride through a night as still and dark as a night could be. John favoured the northerly ride in order to find Furnace Creek and trace it back to the ruin where their own horses were.

Very little was said until they smelled the source of Furnace Creek where they turned southward, paralleled the creek until the pre-dawn chill arrived and later, with day breaking, saw the adobe ruin and reached it as the sun was barely clear of the earth's curve in the east.

Their bedrolls and cooking pans were where they had left them. Tom favoured turning their own horses loose and keeping the big cavalry horses until John

Furnace Creek

pointed put that the army horses had a conspicuous US brand on their necks which was clearly visible because the mane of each horse was trained to fall on the opposite side. As John said, from here on their trail was likely to be through territories inhabited by people suspicious of strangers. They didn't need horses with an army brand under them.

Tom went after their horses and returned carrying the hobbles. The boy explored the ruin. He was hungry – they all were – but John freed the big army animals, seemed in no particular hurry because since leaving the Indians he wondered about something. He sat down with the saddle-bags between his legs and opened them. Tom was looking over his shoulder and said, 'Son – of – a – bitch!'

John said nothing, just sat there. Eventually he looked up. 'I thought they was too heavy. Paper money don't weigh much.' He lifted one of the magnificent, solid gold crucifixes and held it toward the window hole where daylight shone.

There was more. Gold coins and jewelry. Tom knelt to look as he said, 'That old screwt. I hope to hell he made it. What'll we do with this stuff?'

John wagged his head. One thing was a lead-pipe cinch, they could not dispose of the plunder in any of the places he had been. 'Take it along,' he said, and replaced the crucifix, buckled straps in place and stood up.

Tom said, 'It'll be nice to ride saddles again. You ready?'

John nodded as the boy returned from his exploration and said, 'There's a cellar with some old-time In'ian things in it. Masks an' a sort of notched stick for a ladder to get down in it.'

John stood with the saddle-bags over one shoulder looking at the boy. Until this moment he hadn't thought of anything except getting away from the border country. The boy stood looking straight back. Until this moment he also hadn't thought of anything but getting away from the Indians. Now, he and the older man stonily regarded one another until Tom poked his head through the door opening to say, 'You ready? The horses is.'

John jerked his head. 'We'll get you a saddle directly.'

They left the ruin riding warily, avoiding fields of boulders and clumps of trees. The farther north they rode the more morning sun brightened an empty terrain as far as they could see. Once when they stopped to rest because the heat was increasing the lad pointed eastward and said, 'That's where I come from.'

Tom looked, as far as he could see there was nothing but open country interspersed with fields of huge rocks and an occasional stand of trees. He looked at the boy, 'We'll take you home,' he said.

The boy seemed to almost visibly cringe as he looked at John and spoke in a tight voice. 'I want to ride with you.'

John nodded. Tom might have objected but Tom did not know about the lad's stepfather so John spoke first. 'Glad to have you along, Frank.'

When they were again on the trail Tom rode close to speak softly to his partner. 'What're we goin' to do with the boy?'

'Take him along.'

'What the hell are you talkin' about? We can't take

Furnace Creek

him with us.'

'Until we find a decent place to leave him,' John replied and kneed his horse ahead, up where the boy was riding, interested in everything he saw.

John had reason to remember an unhappy childhood not much different than the lad's. He worried a chew off his plug, which was almost down to nothing by now, and rode beside the lad in easy conversation. Once he glanced back. Tom shook his head.

They rode half the night, bedded down near a coldwater spring, left the horses to graze hobbled and even made a tiny fire to boil water in, with jerky.

It was an excellent meal as almost any meal is when previous meals have been postponed. They rode comfortably before the sun climbed very high, and saw their first riders. There were three of them sitting on a low ridge watching John and his companions. They had no idea how long they had been watching. Tom said they looked like stockmen, but at that distance that was a guess, a reasonable one though because they had been passing through cattle country since the night before.

They passed the watchers from about a half-mile. The did not raise the customary wave and neither did the watchers on their low rim.

The next time they halted they had a small village in sight easterly about a mile. Tom took one of their greenbacks from the saddle-bags and loped in that direction for tinned food. John and Frank selected a little spit of oaks to set up camp. The horses grazed in grass nearly knee high. It was making seed heads, which John thought was early in the season, forgetting that in semi-arid country most plants head-up early.

Frank wondered about those men they had seen. So

did John but avoided talking about it. They talked of many things, the boy's mother, his stepfather, about the ranch he was leaving, and he asked John questions a boy would ask and which an outlaw mostly could not answer without evasion. Other questions he could, talk about wild horses, wild Mexican cattle which could come close to outrunning a horse, about areas the lad had never seen. Not once did Frank mention a destination, which pleased the older man because he did not have a destination. A dream but not a destination.

Tom returned with half a croaker-sack full of tinned food. They made another small fire and this time they had salt beef to put in their cooking pot. The coffee to be boiled after the meat had been shared and the pan scoured.

Tom said the village had one store that carried everything from fine harness to bolt goods for dresses. He said the place was called Mimsville and did not seem to have more than a couple hundred inhabitants. He also mentioned four roads that passed through Mimsville, one each from the four compass points.

Frank rolled in early. John and Tom sat by the little fire over black coffee. They had something in particular to discuss. John mentioned it first by saying, 'If you figure to go east you're gettin' farther'n farther off course.'

Tom delayed his reply until he'd finished the coffee then he said, 'That's why I brought the croaker-sack back with me. We can divvy up tomorrow can't we?'

10
INTERFERENCE

With the first blush of a new day they sent the boy southward to scout for riders. He left happy to be given a responsible job. John opened his saddle-bags; Tom opened his croaker-sack. They counted out the money first, in two stacks, then almost indifferently divided the plunder old Mexican Horse had put in the saddle-bags, not because they were not aware of its value but because they both knew they couldn't even trade it for food in any of the territories they were familiar with.

As Tom rigged out with the sack tied on one side of his saddle he said, 'Tell the boy goodbye for me . . . John? You goin' to keep him with you?'

'Until I figure out what to do with him,' John replied.

Tom smiled slightly. 'I don't feel so bad leavin' then. You still got a partner.'

When the lad returned to report that he had seen no riders behind them, he looked around, saw only two horses and asked about Tom. John was rigging out with his back to the lad when he answered, 'He left. We figured to split up.'

'Where will he go?'

John finished saddling and replied almost casually, 'Easterly. I think he has kin or friends somewhere in that direction.'

As they started riding Frank said, 'Won't you miss him, bein' partners an' all?'

John looked straight ahead when he replied. 'Son, in this life you meet folks you cotton to. People are like autumn leaves, they come into your life an' they go out of it; it goes on as far as I know for as long as you live.'

They rode a mile before the lad spoke without looking at John. 'You'n me could be partners?'

John smiled and nodded.

They passed villages and one fairly large town and kept on riding. John knew in which direction they were travelling without knowing much else. They were miles easterly of the Furnace Creek country, land he had never seen before.

There were bands of cattle which only fled if the riders got too close, and twice they saw large bands of mustangs, which did not wait to see if the riders were coming in their direction, but scuffed up clouds of dust as they raced out of sight.

It was hot so they halted in mid-afternoon where there was a sweetwater-creek. The horses grazed hobbled, John and the boy napped in tree shade. Once when one of their horses nickered John roused up.

There were three riders side by side, looking in the direction of their camp with backgrounding trees behind them. John rubbed his eyes. He could not be sure but it could have been the same three horsemen they had seen the day before, far southward, but John scoffed at himself for suspecting that. They had covered

Furnace Creek

a lot of miles between places. Those watchers near the trees were just rangemen.

By the time he and the boy had eaten and the horses were full as ticks, they were ready to ride again. The sun was sliding away but the heat was still strong enough to create heat waves which they rode through heading north.

John did not intend to keep to this course, the farther north he went the closer he got to territory where he was not wanted.

The following day he changed course above a town with big shade trees and brick buildings, which they did not enter nor even go near.

Frank did not question their change of course. He was happy to be astride seeing new country in John Beeson's company. Boy-like, he gave no thought about the man riding beside him beyond the fact that they got along well. He liked John. He had not liked Tom very much.

Several times after they changed course the lad saw John twist in the saddle looking back. The last time John did that was when daylight was falling.

They rode into the night seeking water and feed. There was grass in abundance but creeks were few and far between. This night they had to make a dry camp. John told the boy that in strange country to always remember to make camp next to water even if it was in the middle of the day, which was in effect a matter of admonishing himself because he had not obeyed this first rule of travelling horsemen. The reason was simple. The last time he had looked back he had distantly seen three horsemen riding abreast down their back trail. Not hastening, just riding steadily and inexorably.

Furnace Creek

The following morning when they struck camp John angled toward some timbered uplands. They had no particular destination anyway so losing time did not matter.

Leaving tracks did matter.

They worked their way through huge old over-ripe pines and firs until John found a little point, left the boy minding the horses and went out there. The view was panoramic but he was not interested in something spectacular, he was interested in three riders following their tracks without haste but with an almost unnerving persistence.

Near the end of the day John again broke the first rule of horsemen in strange country. He remained in the timber where pine and fir needles six inches thick did not take imprints well, particularly because of forest gloom, and continued to ride until the foothill timber thinned out and eventually went back down to open country without even hesitating.

If Frank wondered he said nothing, but along toward midnight he fell asleep in the saddle. John rode onward until they came across an old wooden watering trough fed by a hollowed sapling which fed water to the trough from an uphill spring, and stopped.

Frank slept under his saddle blanket almost as soon as he was on the ground. The smell of cattle was strong in this place. John guessed it was probably the only watering place for some miles.

The trough leaked a little, mostly it overflowed which made marshy ground with cropped-short grass around it.

He cared for the animals, wrapped himself in his bedroll and leaned against a flourishing cottonwood

Furnace Creek

tree, the only tree around.

But along toward dawn he fell asleep. What awakened him was Frank bringing in the horses with hobbles slung over his shoulder.

The lad was hungry. As John would learn, although the boy never complained, when he finally had a chance to eat he put away enough food to fill a grown man.

They did not make a fire, ate their fill, rigged out and left the old wooden trough. John sought a place for cover, eventually found a grassy arroyo, rode down into it, left the lad with the horses and climbed back to lie flat on the rim.

They were coming out of the trees toward the trough. They were too distant for him to see them in detail but he did not require that; he was satisfied they were following them.

They left the arroyo angling northward again toward side hills which had stumps where once big trees had stood. It was poor cover but until full daylight arrived they would probably be unseen.

John saw Frank looking at him and smiled. The boy said, 'We bein' dogged?'

John nodded and the lad rode twisted in the saddle, looking back. When he saw horsemen following their back-trail he sat forward. 'Why?' he asked. 'Who are they?'

John had no idea who they were but he told Frank they had been following them for a couple of days, maybe longer but he hadn't been sure.

Their attention was distracted by cattle being herded southward by two riders. If those men saw John and Frank they were too occupied with half-wild cattle to heed them or even wave.

They encountered more cattle, small bands of them, and only once did they square around in a challenging stance, that was when they were cows with baby calves.

John veered around them on a wide trail. Several of the cows lowered their heads and pawed dirt. Frank said, 'They'll charge us.'

John did not think so. 'Not when they got little calves. They won't do more'n make a few rushes.'

He was right, several of the cattle bawled, threw up their heads and made short runs. John and Frank were too distant to worry, but the boy kept watching the cows even after they were far behind.

Two riders appeared from the foothills, halted, evidently in surprise, then eased forward in John and Frank's direction. They had been flushing the foothills for cattle, a routine chore in wolf and bear country.

They were well mounted. Like the riders far back they did not hasten as they angled to make an interception.

John's breath caught up short before he said, 'That there one out front is a woman.'

He was correct. When the pair of riders drew rein waiting for John and the lad to come up it was easy to see that one was indeed a woman. She was dressed like a rider except for the hair which showed below the brim of her hat. She was rawboned without any spare weight and sat her saddle with gloved hands resting atop the horn in the manner of someone of assurance.

Where they came together the dark man beside the woman said, 'Howdy. We figured you might be ranch riders – exceptin' for this one. He's pretty young.'

John smiled slightly. 'Just passin' through.'

Furnace Creek

The woman spoke. Her voice was soft but firm. She ignored John and asked Frank his name.

He told her, and because of the way the woman and her companion stared, Frank was uncomfortable so he also said, 'We been ridin' some time.'

The woman said, 'Have you? Where from?'

Frank looked at John who answered. 'Down south a ways.'

Her gaze was fixed on John like the eyes of a snake. 'Long ride,' she said, and when John nodded, she also said, 'You passed a town yestiddy.'

John nodded again, no longer smiling. They had passed a number of towns. He was beginning to have an uncomfortable premonition. The woman's next words reinforced it. She said, 'Is your name John Beeson?'

Frank saw his partner pale a little, and John did not answer the question but nodded his head.

'That town you passed, Mister Beeson, 's got a telegraph . . . the army wants to talk to you.'

John looked at the boy, who was biting his lip. He said, 'Don't fret, Frank. They'll want to know about the In'ians is all.'

The boy suddenly said, 'Ma'am he don't want to talk to the army 'n neither do I.'

The woman's grey eyes showed a faint glimmer of hard humour when she looked at the boy. 'All I said was that the army's telegraphin' around about talkin' of Mister Beeson. You'd ought to know that.' She returned her attention to John. 'We figured it'd be you because of the lad. Now you know, Mister Beeson.' She was shortening her reins when someone yelled from the rearward distance.

Furnace Creek

John turned so fast his spine shot pain up to his shoulders. It was a solitary rider not three of them and the closer the man got the more John was satisfied he had never seen him before.

The woman and her dark companion watched the oncoming horseman. The man said, 'Got a burr under his blanket.'

The woman said nothing as the rider slackened and covered the last few hundred feet looking at John and the boy. When he came up his attention was on the woman. 'Me'n Roy got about thirty head on their way. Three fellers met us at the trough, said they was deputy marshals an' they was after some feller who's maybe two, three miles ahead ridin' with a kid.'

The woman gazed at the rangeman for a silent moment, then said, 'Did they have badges?'

'Well; me'n Roy had no reason to ask. They're hard-lookin' individuals.'

The woman briefly hung fire again before addressing John. 'Someone been down your back trail, Mister Beeson?'

John nodded. 'Three riders.'

'Do you know them?'

'No ma'am, they never got close enough for us to get a look at them.'

'How long have they been doggin' you?'

'Two, three days.'

The woman looked at her dark companion. He looked back and said, 'Suppose they is federal lawmen, Mrs Dexter?'

'Then bring them to the yard. Blaze, if they aren't – if they're some kind of bounty hunters for the army, or someone else like that . . . .' She did not finish the sen-

Furnace Creek

tence and the dark man reined away taking the other rangeman with him.

The woman spoke to John. 'Come with me. We'll wait for Blaze at the yard.' As she reined around she also said, 'I'm a widow, Mister Beeson. My husband and son were killed seven years ago come August. Is the boy your son, Mister Beeson?'

'No, ma'am.'

'Then how's it come he's riding with you?'

John and Frank rode with the woman. As they went along John said, 'It's a long story.'

The widow-woman was not a person to be put off. She raised a gloved hand. 'You see the cottonwoods yonder?'

John saw them, they appeared to be several miles distant. They were the only large trees in the direction they were riding. She lowered her arm and curtly said, 'We got plenty of time, Mister Beeson.'

John and Frank exchanged a glance before John told her their story beginning with John and Tom's capture by Mexican Horse's renegades. Before he had finished they not only had the big old trees in sight but also the yard and buildings.

It was a big cow outfit. The trees shaded a large yard and part of a log barn beyond which were a number of outbuildings and the main house.

She led them to the big barn, swung off with only a glance at the boy, began pulling the latigo loose as she said, 'Get down.'

They dismounted. Young Frank was thoroughly intimidated by the woman. If she'd told him to jump he would have asked her how high.

They stalled the animals in the barn, forked feed to

them and followed the woman across a brickhard yard where nothing grew to the main house. She showed them where to sit and went inside. Frank leaned to speak softly to John.

'She's more man than female-woman, ain't she?'

John nodded, considered the large yard, the buildings and wondered if she ramrodded this place by herself. She did and eventually he would understand why.

She brought John watered whiskey and a glass of sarsaparilla for the boy. She said her name was Mary Dexter, sat down and gently rocked as she too looked across the yard. 'It'll be a spell,' she told them, and faced John. Under the wide overhang which was never without shadow, she still looked as hard as nails but she also looked younger. 'Do you know if the In'ians got down into Messico, Mister Beeson?'

He didn't. 'No ma'am. Like I told you we lit out while the fight was still goin' on.'

'You didn't fight the soldiers?'

'No, ma'am.'

She faintly frowned. 'You run out on the In'ians?'

John coloured a little. 'Like I said, Messican Horse wasn't no one you argued with. He was real strong about tellin' us to leave.'

'Were you'n him friends, Mister Beeson?'

'Well, I expect we was. My partner'n me helped 'em a little.'

She changed the direction of their conversation. 'Why are three men following you?'

'I got no idea. Like I said before, we was never close enough to get a good look at 'em.'

The woman squinted into the distance, so did John. They saw nothing but John thought they should have

Furnace Creek

seen riders by now so he said, 'The odds was three to two, Missus Dexter.'

She smiled without humour. 'You don't know my rangeboss, Mister Beeson' She did not say more.

Frank finished his sarsaparilla and fell asleep in the chair. The woman said, 'Carry him inside, Mister Beeson,' and led the way to a musty-smelling, gloomy bedroom whose window shutters hadn't been opened in years.

John put the boy on the bed as the woman opened the shutters. In good light John saw this had once been a youngster's bedroom. He watched the woman cover the lad and followed her back to the long, wide porch where she sat in a rocking chair and looked steadily and silently northward.

John assumed she was watching for riders and when he saw them in the blurry, heat-hazed distance he said, 'Yonder; they're coming.'

His sudden words made the woman start in her chair. She hadn't been looking for riders, she had been on a journey back down the years.

She briefly rocked. When she recognized her dark rangeboss she arose, moved to the railing and stood there as straight as though she had a ramrod up her back.

John joined her, but was more relaxed. There were five riders. He assumed – correctly – two of them were the dark man and the other Dexter rider. He was right.

She asked if John recognized the other three. He had to shake his head, the distance was too great for a detailed identification, but fifteen minutes later he said, 'I'll be damned.'

Mary Dexter frowned at him. 'Didn't your maw tell

you not to use bad language in front of women?'

John coloured slightly. 'Sorry, ma'am – but that hefty feller ridin' next to your rangeboss . . . .'

'What about him?'

'I don't recollect his name if I ever heard it but I'd know that face, beard an' all in my sleep. He was one of the prisoners I told you about.'

John hesitated until the horsemen were entering the north end of the yard, then he said, 'They was with the bearded feller. There's supposed to be another one. There were four, like I told you.'

Mary Dexter remained standing in overhang shade clearly visible to the oncoming riders. She still looked like she had a ramrod up her back. Her profile, which was all John could see, had a set to the jaw which was unmistakable.

The dark man veered toward the tie-rack in front of the barn, growled for everyone to get down and tie their animals, then growled again as he and the other Dexter rider walked on each side of the strangers in the direction of the porch where the woman was standing.

11
A TRADE

When the bearded man saw John he did not smile but he said, 'You done them In'ians proud.'

The woman's gaze was cold when she spoke. 'What's your name, whiskers?'

The bearded man's sunk-set grey eyes lingered on the woman stare for stare. 'It's George Washington, ma'am.'

The dark man struck with the speed of a rattler. The bearded man went down to his knees, did not utter a sound, wavered briefly then stood up. He ignored the dark man who had hit him. 'Ma'am, that feller beside you is an outlaw. We're here to take him away.'

Mary Dexter's gaze was sardonic. 'Is that a fact, Mister Washington? You don't do anythin' on the Dexter place unless I say for you to . . . outlaw? An' what are you, Mister Washington, a federal marshal?'

Furnace Creek

The bearded man took his time answering. He had taken the measure of Mary Dexter – solid iron all the way through. He rubbed his neck where the rangeboss's blow had landed as he replied. 'We ain't outlaws. We rode with a cowman after some renegade tomahawks. He was with 'em. In fact he helped 'em get to the border. When the fight broke out him an' another man an' the boy run for it. After the fight the soldiers turned us loose.'

The dark rangeboss said, 'They're ridin' US-branded horses.'

Mary Dexter's gaze was fixed on the bearded man. 'Are those men with you federal marshals too?'

The way she asked that made it clear she was being sarcastic. Another of the stained, unwashed men, who was fine-boned and pale-eyed spoke. 'Ma'am, my name's Richard Helm. His name is Jeff Barlow. This other feller's Ames Burton. What Jeff told you's the truth. That feller beside you run off when the fight started.'

Mary Dexter considered the man with watery pale eyes. He was definitely different from the other two. She did not address the bearded man again. 'Mister Helm, how did you get those army horses?'

'The In'ians got around 'em in the dark, set some of them free and we caught those we were riding.'

'And did Mister Beeson run out on the In'ians?'

'All I know is that the In'ian, feller called Mexican Horse, put him, his partner and a boy on horses, give 'em their goods and drove them off.'

'You saw all this?'

'Yes'm.'

'Mister Helm, are you a federal lawman?'

Furnace Creek

The thin, haggard-looking man was a poor liar. He hung fire before answering, 'Yes'm.'

'You got a badge, have you?'

The only man who had not yet spoken broke in when the thin man hesitated again. This was the man called Ames Burton. 'Lady, he's got somethin' we got a right to. Look in his saddle-bags. We been doggin' him to get it back.'

The woman put her flinty gaze on Ames Burton. 'What does he have of yours?'

The bearded man would have answered but the woman said, 'Be quiet. Mister Burton, what does he have?'

'We seen the old In'ian put some things in his saddle bags, an –'

'And it belonged to you?'

'Yes'm.'

'What is it, Mister Burton?'

The bearded man strained to reply. The rangeboss caught him by the neck and exerted pressure.

Ames Burton replied, 'Some gold crosses, some gold coins, other things.'

Mary Dexter's sardonic gaze was fixed on Ames Burton. 'Federal marshals after plunder?'

It was too late for the bearded man to take the initiative. He looked at the ground then slowly turned to look at Ames Burton. He had never doubted that Ames was born with one foot out of the stirrup, but he took orders well, made a good hang-rope posse rider.

Burton stood looking up at the woman on the porch, He knew he had walked into a trap but wasn't sure exactly how. He remained silent.

Mary Dexter made a little gesture before speaking to

Furnace Creek

her rangeboss. 'Take them to the woodshed, search 'em real good. I'll decide later what to do with them.'

The bearded man would have spoken but the rangeboss took him by the arm in a vice-like grip, yanked him around and led off toward a distant open-fronted shed.

Mary Dexter was watching them go and did not look around when she spoke to John Beeson. 'What's in your saddle-bags?' She turned to face John.

He had told her about Mexican Horse putting plunder in his saddle-bags but he told her again, and this time made a proposal.

'They can have it. If they're caught with that stuff they'll be in trouble up to their ears.'

'Do you want to part with it?'

'Like I just said, ma'am, anyone'd know it's stolen stuff. Farther south they'd know it come from Mex churches and big ranches.'

'What's it worth?'

'I got no idea but I'd say a lot of money.'

'And you'd give it to them.'

'Yes'm, just to know when they went to sell it the sky would fall in on 'em.'

'I'd like to see it.'

John nodded. 'The bags is on my saddle.'

'Get it, bring it to the house. I want to look in on the boy. What did you say his name was?'

'Frank Leslie,' John told her and started down off the veranda heading for the barn.

Mary Dexter went inside, but did not go to the bedroom until she'd fired up the cook-stove and made a large mug of hot beef broth which she took to the bedroom with her.

Furnace Creek

Frank was awake and standing by the only window in the room which faced southward. She handed him the mug. He went to the bed, perched on the edge and tried the broth. It was too hot.

The woman went to stand by the window. She spoke without facing around. 'Is Mister Beeson a good man, Frank?'

'Yes. Real nice man.'

'How about your stepfather?'

'No ma'am, he was mean. He'd knock you down just for lookin' at him.'

Mary Dexter went to a chair, sat down with her hands in her lap and smiled. 'Where are you'n Mister Beeson going?'

Frank tried the broth again but it was still too hot. 'Just goin', ma'am. He didn't say an' I expect it don't matter.'

The woman waited until the lad had sipped broth before asking another question. 'Do you figure Mister Beeson run out on those In'ians?'

'No ma'am. The old In'ian boss drove us off.'

'Mister Beeson said the posse-riders you was with cut out in the night, about half of 'em.'

Frank put the half-emptied cup aside. 'The In'ians an' Mister Beeson couldn't figure out why.'

'But you did?'

'I think so. My step-paw was the boss. He was hard on every one of 'em. Mean and ornery. Mostly, those men was good to me. When he knocked me down a couple of times they near' ganged up on him. I think when he told Mister Beeson he didn't care if the In'ians killed me, they just split off and left. Mostly, they'd had enough of him.'

'And you?'

'Yes, ma'am.. I could've gone after them. Mister Beeson said I could.'

'But you wanted to go with Mister Beeson?'

'Yes'm. He's a kindly person. My maw was a kindly person. She smiled a lot when we'd play. Mister Beeson smiles too. '

'No matter where he goes you want to go with him?'

'Yes'm. He said we're partners.'

'How old are you, Frank?'

'Fifteen, my maw said. Every summer she'd make me a dough-cake. She said it was my birthday.'

'What day, Frank?'

The boy fidgeted. 'I told you, summertime.'

She left him when she heard John enter the parlour. Frank drained the cup and returned to looking out the window where the sun was slanting away with shadows forming.

John put the saddle-bags atop a table near a smoke-stained stone fireplace, solemnly dumped everything atop the table and heard the woman draw in quick breath as she looked briefly at the plunder then said, 'The In'ian gave you all that money?'

'No ma'am. Just the gold coins, not the greenbacks.'

'Where did they come from? How much is there?'

'Three thousand dollars. There was all-told six thousand. Tom got half.' She stood looking at the tabletop.

'And Tom's gone?'

'Yes'm. He took some of the plunder with him, but he's too *coyote* to try'n peddle it.'

John had thought she'd ask that and had no quick answer.

She said, 'Outlaw money, Mister Beeson?'

John nodded without speaking or looking at her. 'From where – and how?'

'From up in Wyoming near the Montana line. How – well – from a bank an' a bullion stage.'

Mary Dexter felt for a chair and sat silently regarding the hands in her lap. John stepped over to the fireplace with his back to it, looked at her. 'What I been wonderin', ma'am. Could I leave the boy with you?'

She raised her head slowly She would gladly take the boy but it wouldn't be that simple. She said, 'We talked. Mister Beeson if you left him with me I think he'd saddle up in the night an' try to find you.'

'He's young, Missus Dexter. He's a good boy. You'n him would make out real well an' he'd have a home. Boys need a home.'

'How well do you know him, Mister Beeson?'

'Well, we been together for some time.'

Mary Dexter studied John and remembered something she had thought about her dead husband. Men had a hole in their minds big enough to drive a hitch and a wagon through. She said, 'He's cottoned to you like a father.'

John scratched inside his shirt, gazed at the tabletop where greenbacks lay like scattered leaves. 'I got a bounty on my head. The kind of life I'll lead ain't right for a lad of his age. I got to keep movin', avoid towns, camp on hilltops. Someday I'd like to get a piece of ground, build a house on it, run a few horses'n cows, but that ain't likely. If I settled somewhere, sooner or later they'd find me . . . I'd take it right kindly if you'd take the boy. I'll saddle up an' ride on in the night. You keep him close for a few days. He'll forget. You got everythin' here he needs, mostly a home with decent folks. You understand? One other thing, them three chained in the woodshed . . . remember I got a price on my head.'

Mary Dexter had been shaking her head slightly, long before John had finished speaking. Now, she looked straight at him. 'What did you say your first name is?'

'John.'

'John, a dog might forget in time, or a horse, but not that boy. What he told me about you – like I said, he's got an idea you're the paw he don't have . . . he'd never forget you. Not as long as he lived.'

John raised his eyes to the ceiling and let go a long sigh. Why in tarnation had he taken the boy with him? Well – he had. Mary Dexter arose, went to the table, sorted the gold coins and other plunder from the greenbacks, looked around and said, 'All right; give it to them, get them on their way. You'n the boy stay awhile.'

'Lady, I told you, they know who I am. There's Wanted dodgers on me. Them three would sell their mothers for a lot less'n thirty pieces of silver.'

She smiled at him for the first time. 'Let me take care of that. Now, I'll fix supper for you'n Frank, but first, would you like some whiskey?'

John nodded, watched her go into the kitchen and swore under his breath.

Supper was torment. In the first place Frank ate like a horse, which embarrassed John. In the second place when he spoke he did so almost exclusively by addressing John, who stole a glance or two at the woman. She did not appear to feel slighted, but then John knew just enough about her to suspect whatever she felt she was adept at allowing it not to show.

He brought her into the conversation often. Frank would look at her, even smile, and once he told her he hadn't eaten so well since before his maw died. She liked that so John thought he might still talk her into keeping the boy but moments later the boy was looking at John when he spoke.

After supper John took the boy aside and whispered to him it would be mannerly if he helped Mrs Dexter clean up the kitchen, then John went out front where daylight lingered with dusk in the offing.

He thought about giving the prisoners most of the plunder and was satisfied they would take it and agree to ride away. But the word of men like that was worse than worthless. They'd hunt up the law and return with a posse. At least, he told himself, he could trade the loot for a day or two after they had departed and before they could return with the law.

He was still planning things when Frank came out to the veranda, dropped into a chair and said, 'She didn't need no help. She told me to come out here, keep you company, an' she'd be along later.'

John accepted the lad's presence. It did not dawn on him for a while that the woman had deliberately sent the boy. He was distracted by two men emerging from the bunkhouse heading for the three-sided shed. They had tin plates. Frank said, 'Them fellers in the shed got to be gettin' used to bein' tied up.'

The woman came out. She had brushed her hair. In pre-dusk light she again looked much younger. She handed John a glass of watered whiskey for which he mumbled his thanks.

The Dexter riders emerged from the shed with empty

plates. The woman waited until they were back in the bunkhouse before saying, 'In the morning, John.'

He understood. The boy didn't, but on a full stomach in fascinating surroundings without fear of any kind, he accepted the fact that sometimes grown people spoke in parables, and didn't care.

John's discomfort increased. Every time the boy said something to him he felt like a traitor, but what he had told the woman was for the best of the lad. That did not mitigate the feeling of betraying Frank by riding off in the night.

Mary Dexter told them about her ranch, her riders, she even mentioned her late husband but skipped over that as though even after seven years it was difficult to talk about him.

She was careful about what she said to John, which left him feeling grateful even though he figured she was making him look a little sagacious, even a mite heroic, for the boy's sake.

By the time they were ready to turn in John had developed a respect for the woman he hadn't even felt for a lot of men. She was shrewd and understanding. She was also both compassionate and hard as iron. He could not imagine anyone deceiving her.

Frank was the last one to arise the following morning. Sleeping up off the ground in a regular bed did that to folks, even the young whose boundless energy and curiosity normally awakened them early.

The rangeboss and Mary Dexter finished a discussion on the veranda when John appeared. She smiled, told him to roust the boy out, she had the griddle hot and the bacon warming.

When they finished eating the rangeboss returned

with two Dexter riders and the three prisoners. She told Frank to go with the rangeboss, help do the barn chores. After he and her rider departed Mary Dexter's jaw assumed the unrelenting slant as she led the way to the parlour.

John got a jolt. Part of the plunder was still atop the table, about two-thirds of it in fact. Most of the greenbacks and the gold coins were gone.

Mary Dexter asked the beard-stubbled, unwashed men if they had been fed. They had, all the beans and mashed potatoes they could hold, washed down with black java.

She stood stiff and unsmiling when she looked in John's direction. He took the cue and addressed the bearded man with the deep-set grey eyes.

'You see what's on the table?'

All three men had barely glanced at Mary Dexter or John. They were staring at the plunder. The bearded man nodded but did not speak until John said, 'Take it and be on your way.'

The bearded man looked long at John. 'Why?'

'So's you'll be satisfied an' don't tell no one I was here.'

The bearded man looked from John to Mary Dexter and back before speaking to John. 'Is that all of it?'

'Mostly. Some pieces ain't there but that's most of it.'

The bearded man went to the table. His companions did the same. They touched nothing, just looked until John said, 'Your horse's been fed,' and the bearded man turned slowly. 'You want to ride with us?'

John coldly smiled. 'I'm goin' out of this country alone, as far as I can get . . . well?'

The bearded man smiled and relaxed. When he

picked up the first piece and pocketed it his companions did the same using both hands, their discomfort at being chained in the woodshed forgotten. They even smiled a little. The bearded man turned to face John. He had a pensive expression on his face. 'I'll tell you mister, as far as I'm concerned I never saw you after the border fight.'

John nodded. 'Goodbye an' good luck.'

Mary Dexter went to the porch with the trio and called to the barn for their horses to be saddled. She also called the rangeboss to the porch. John could not distinguish what they talked about but as the dark man started toward the steps his last words were distinguishable. He said, 'I'll tell 'em.'

Mary Dexter returned to the parlour, glanced a little ruefully at the table where the plunder had been and went to a chair before speaking to John.

'I been judging men since my husband died. There's been plenty come visiting.' She made a wry small smile. 'I'd say the whiskered feller meant what he said about not seeing you. But those other two, I wouldn't bet money on what they'd do.'

John heard Frank on the veranda and swiftly said, 'It won't matter. I'm an old hand at disappearin'.'

Mary Dexter looked steadily at John until the boy came in, then asked if Frank had helped her men at the barn. His face was flushed, his eyes were bright. 'That In'ian-lookin' feller –'

'His name is Blaze. He's my rangeboss.'

'Yes'm. Well, he said I was a good worker.'

John watched the boy in silence until Mary Dexter arose to get the coffee. Then she said, 'Frank . . . you're welcome to stay.'

The boy's brightness faded. He looked at John when he addressed her. 'Both of us, ma'am.'

12
THE MATTER OF PARTNERS

Frank slept in the house. John bedded down at the bunkhouse. He lay awake a long time. The boy's last words before they parted bore out what the woman had said: Frank had cottoned to John as though they were father and son.

He heaved up on his side. Someone was snoring, another man in the dark cleared his pipes.

John could easily get away from here. It was a dark night, his horse was refreshed, By morning he could be in those mountains to the north. After that the lad couldn't track him very well if at all.

He fell asleep in the midst of his idea and when he awakened two men were rassling breakfast and arguing about how much longer the coffee was going to last.

He dressed, went out back to clean up and saw two lights at the main house: one a kitchen light, the other a parlour light.

As he scrubbed and shaved he was angry with himself for having fallen asleep. He had a good excuse: yesterday had been not only a long day, but it had also been one of those times when a man's nerves remained taut as a bowstring. Nothing wore a man out as much as being tight-wound for hours on end.

He ate with the riders. Breakfast, fortunately, was the one meal of the day when conversation was minimal. The riders left one at a time heading for the corral and barn. John sluiced off his eating utensils like the others had done and was leaving the bunkhouse when the boy called to him from the veranda.

He went over there to be greeted by a broad smile as Frank led him indoors. Mary Dexter was cleaning up in the kitchen. She came to the doorway wearing an apron and holding a knotted dish towel. He said, 'Morning, ma'am.'

She smiled slightly and returned the greeting, then beckoned him to the kitchen, which smelled wonderfully of fried meat and hash-browns.

She put two cups of coffee on the table on opposite sides, nodded to Frank who went outside to fill the wood box as the woman sat down. John dutifully sat opposite her, she wasted no time on the niceties which were customary in cow country. She got right to the point. 'I need another rider,' she said.

John was doubtful of that. According to what he had seen she had a full crew.

'Regular pay, Saturday'n Sunday off.'

He cupped both hands around the coffee mug and ruefully smiled at her. 'Just keep the boy, ma'am. Don't fret about me. I've been lookin' –'

'You're thicker'n oak, Mister Beeson. That lad would leave the first chance he got. An' he'd find you, I don't care how *coyote* you are, he's smart. He'd find you.

Furnace Creek

That's not altogether the reason why I'll hire you on. The other reason is that Blaze an' another feller are going to track those manhunters because I got a suspicion they didn't go very far. Dexter ranch is big and isolated. We've been raided before. Mister Beeson, Blaze agrees with me – they'll be out there waitin' for you to ride by.'

John sipped coffee. She was a direct, iron-willed woman. He put the cup down looking straight at her. 'Them three can foller a trail, an' they stay on it, but I've out-ridden an' out-shinnied my share of posse riders.'

'And what about the boy?' she asked.

John had been over this ground several times with her, and he really did not like abandoning the lad even to her who'd give him a good home, so he flared up at her. 'You got to be deef or the most pig-headed woman I ever met. Leave me out of it. Keep the lad, keep him busy, be good to him. He'll forget.'

She reddened. 'I can't chain him every night an' even if I could I wouldn't do it.'

John drained the cup and got to his feet. Before he could speak she said, 'I'm not being pig-headed, you are. You don't know a damned thing about children so let me tell you . . . .'

John stamped out of the kitchen, slammed the front door, went down to the barn, rigged out his horse, got astride and did not look back. If he had he would have seen the woman, erect as a pole, watching him leave the yard, and at her side was the boy.

He said, 'Where's he goin'?'

She answered shortly, 'I don't know. '

Furnace Creek

'Is he comin' back?'

The woman did not reply. She saw John lift his horse into a lope and put a gentle hand on Frank's shoulder. 'You can help me gather eggs.' Frank followed her outside and down past the barn to the hen house. He walked behind her staring northward where John Beeson was small in the distance, still loping. When the woman was inside the chicken yard the boy slammed the gate and latched the hasp from the outside with a halter snap and ran to the barn.

Mary Dexter lunged for the gate. The fence was six feet high and solid. Like most chicken yards it had been constructed to keep varmints out.

She called Frank, pleaded with him, frantically looked for a way out of the yard, ended up behind the gate calling, struggling with the gate and, when he loped past, she called, 'Frank, let him go. He wanted you to stay here. So do I . . . Frank!'

The boy waved, yelled something she could not understand and left the yard in a high lope.

The sun was climbing but the morning remained chilly. Far northward in the forested uplands a thin spiral of smoke rose straight up.

John angled westerly so as to reach the high country several miles west. He had no idea who owned that fire but whoever it was he intended to avoid them.

The range was miles of grassland with only an occasional stand of trees. He saw cattle and they saw him. In this kind of country visibility was excellent. Anything moving caught their attention. The cattle had reason to be wary of anyone on horseback, all their benefits as well as their tribulations came from mounted

Furnace Creek

men. As long as John's course remained wide of their bedding and grazing grounds they watched but did not scatter.

It was the second rider that spooked them. He was indifferent to the cattle, was obviously trying to overtake the first rider, rode too close and scattered several bands of cattle.

He made good time because the rider he was trying to overtake rode at a steady walk, slouched in the saddle with his unhappy thoughts.

He did not even know someone was gaining on him until some spooked cattle made the earth reverberate. He did not draw rein but he twisted with a hand on the cantle.

For a long moment he could only make out the fact that someone was trying to overtake him. The distance prevented him from making out who it was.

He thought of young Frank, settled forward and veered in the direction of the forested foothills. He did not hasten; no fifteen year old would catch John Beeson if he did not want to be caught.

When he reached the trees he blended with their gloom, turned abruptly easterly and watched his pursuer lope past going west. Other times when he eluded pursuit he had smiled. This time he did not smile. In fact he did not feel any elation at all. He was riding among big trees wondering why Mary Dexter hadn't had enough sense to mind the boy better until John was out of the country when a man on a dun horse materialized among the trees like a ghost. John was startled. The interceptor said, 'Get off the horse an' shuck that sidearm.'

John was frozen in the saddle. The other man cocked the six-gun he had been holding in his lap. '*Get down!*'

John swung off trailing one hand. The other man looked straight at Beeson as he said, 'You didn't think we'd leave you with all them gold coins'n greenbacks did you?' He leaned to also dismount. He was looking at the saddle-bags behind John's saddle which was his first mistake. His second mistake was to be on the right side of John's horse when he dismounted.

John recognized the man. He was the bounty-hunter called Ames Burton. John had a short moment to act. He drew, aimed and fired.

The unexpected explosion made both horses wheel in terror and run. The dun horse went eastward, John's horse snorted like a wild boar as he fled back the way he had come.

Ames Burton's knees buckled. He did not fall, he drew and fired. John felt the pain like an explosion throughout his body. Impact drove him against a large tree as he cocked and fired his second shot. This time Ames Burton went over backwards lost his handgun and briefly writhed then became still. The first slug had hit him in the lower body. The second one struck him squarely in the centre of the brisket. He was dead before he lost his six-gun.

John felt blood while the shock still prevented the pain. He had been shot in the upper right leg. He dropped his Colt, fumbled to remove his belt, lashed it tightly above the wound, continued tightening it until the blood dried up to just a slow-spreading leak and sagged against the tree. He began to slide down it and ended up in a sitting position. The pain came. Not gradually but all at once.

He closed his eyes which seemed to make the pain worse so he opened them. He could see through the trees toward rangeland. He recalled waiting for a man to die in Idaho when he'd been young and their hold-up had gone bad. That time too they had been miles from a town and almost as far from a set of buildings they had seen on their ride to the rendezvous in which his partner had been shot.

He remembered every detail, how he had carried the wounded man to safety tied in the saddle, and when they were safe for the moment how he had helped the man down. His legs would not support him so John had carried him to a shelter of tan rocks and propped him in the shade.

The man bled out internally. He did not seem in pain. In fact he smiled. John had been young then and had thought of himself and others like him as being immortal.

The dying man said, 'John-boy, sooner or later the odds get too big. Sell my horse'n outfit an' get yourself a job in town, settle in. The odds'll get you too if you don't.'

The man died slowly, seemed to go to sleep with his eyes open.

His first shot had hit Ames Burton through the body too. John gazed at the corpse and spoke unsteadily to the dead man, 'The odds .... T'tell you the truth, I wasn't sure before but I am now.'

He heard a horse running somewhere easterly. It wasn't a loose horse, it had a rider and he was leaving the country as fast as he could angling toward flat ground away from the uplands. That, John told himself tiredly, was either the bearded man or the other one, the skinny, watery-eyed one.

He lost consciousness for better than an hour. When he opened his eyes there was a horse tied to a tree. He stared at it.

A quavery voice on his right said, 'I caught your horse. He's tied back a-ways.' Frank came around where John could see him. He smiled as the lad said, 'I got to get you on the horse. Can you stand up?'

John continued to smile. He still had pain but mostly he felt very tired. He was thinking of that man he had watched die years back when he said, 'No hurry, son. I'll just set for a spell.'

The boy was white to the hairline. 'No. You got to get on the horse. You been shot.' He got one of John's arms across his shoulders, strained then said, 'You got to help. When I lift you shove. Ready?'

John did not shove. 'Let's just wait a spell,' he said.

Frank was insistent. 'Once more. When I lift you shove. *Now!*' The boy was strong but not strong enough. He managed to get John's left side hoisted a little. The pain increased but the lad would not desist so John pushed hard against the tree until he was standing, then he leaned because his sight had flecks of little lights obscuring it.

Frank leaned against the older man as he said, 'Don't slide down. Lean back and brace. I'll fetch the horse.'

John leaned back. His sight was clearing. He watched the boy lead the Dexter horse to him and stand at its head as he said, 'Get hold of the horn. Now lean forward . . . now then hold tight, I'll put your foot in the stirrup. Now, when I push from below you rise up.'

It worked, John was in the saddle but the moment his right leg came down the horse's off side pain swirled upwards. John gripped the horn with both hands and locked his jaws.

Frank led the animal. Twice he had to stop because John was leaning too far to one side.

They got back to John's animal, Frank snugged it up, got astride and picked a pathway among the trees wide enough to allow him to ride beside the wounded man.

As they started to angle toward open country Frank sounded hopeful when he said, 'You're doin' fine but I wish I had a rope to keep you from leanin' so much.'

It was a long ride made longer by the fact that they could not ride out of a walk. The sun was nearly overhead so there was heat, but Frank did not heed it and John was only aware of heat during the moments when he was lucid enough to grip the horn and lock his jaws.

Once he spoke, mumbled words. 'The odds, son. Mind the odds.'

They lacked about half a mile of reaching the yard. That was when John passed out and leaned so far the boy could not push him upright. He fell like a sack of wet grain. Frank got down to use the older man's saddle bags for a pillow and talk to him with a sinking heart. He was still kneeling like that unaware that the Dexter horse had left them in the direction of the yard.

The boy had tears down both cheeks, was unmindful of everything except John. He was sure the older man was dead, was leaning above him with tears falling when someone lifted him from behind and roughly put him aside. Three men stood with their horses behind the man who had got the lad out of the way, his dark features and black eyes intent as he held the blade of a clasp-knife under John's nostrils, leaned down closer then spoke without raising up. 'Bring a wagon; be quick about it. Tell Missus Dexter he's a bloody mess but alive. *Go!*'

The two riders were about to get astride when Frank tugged at the skirt of a saddle, the rider extended his arm, hoisted the boy behind the cantle and they both rode hard for the yard.

John opened his eyes, saw the dark man above and said, 'Messican Horse?'

The rangeboss rocked back on his heels regarding the wounded man. 'Who shot you?'

'Tom; go scout – take Scar.'

The rangeboss was still cocked back on his heels when the wagon full of timothy hay arrived. With it were the riders, the boy and Mary Dexter. On the side Frank had told her what had happened. She looked as grim as death. As the men lifted John into the wagon she shook her head a little. He could out-think pursuers, knew all the tricks of an outlaw did he? She told the driver to mind bumps and rode beside the wagon right up to the steps of the veranda, then dismounted and led the way inside to a sun-lighted bedroom where she told them to leave him, take care of her horse and send the boy to her.

When John came around again someone was spooning hot beef broth into him. He looked up. Frank said, 'If you move I'll spill it.'

Furnace Creek

He stopped moving, dutifully swallowed and gradually looked around the room. When the broth was gone he said, 'Where is this place, Frank?'

'Missus Dexter's room. She'd done bandaging your leg an' all. You're swole up like a poisoned hawg.'

From the doorway a straight-backed, unsmiling woman said, 'The bleeding's stopped I cleaned the wound while you was unconscious. Frank an' I gave you a good washing, which you needed. The saddlebags are under the bed.'

She came into the room, sat on the edge of the bed and regarded him wryly. 'Mister Beeson, you aren't goin' to set a horse for six months, maybe longer. Which one of 'em was waitin' for you out yonder?'

'The one called Burton.'

She accepted that and said, 'My riders saw another man riding like the wind eastward. That could have been either of them, except that I don't believe it was the bearded one.'

She stood up. To Frank she looked satisfied when she said, 'Six months at the least, Mister Beeson.'

It annoyed him the way she had said that but the only rejoinder he could think of was to say, 'I told you, my name's John! You want me to paint it on the wall for you!'

Her smile lingered. 'Not for six months – John – maybe for eight months. The bone's broken. Blaze an' I set it. If you even think about putting that leg on the floor . . . we did the best we knew to do, we set the bone straight, but a medicine man'd likely splint it, which we didn't do because we figured you wouldn't need more'n the tight bandage, unless you try to get up

155

too soon, then it'll bust loose all over again. Frank, let's go make cookies, he don't look real happy.'

As the woman left the room the boy lingered at the bedside, lay a hand lightly on John's arm and said, 'You was comin' back, wasn't you, because partners don't run out on partners?'

John smiled. 'I come back, didn't I? Frank, I owe you, boy.'

'Naw. Partners help partners. Now I got to go. '

ET